THE COTTONWOOD

Phillip Derrick Hampton

This book is a work of fiction. Names, characters, incidents and places are of pure imagination and are of a fictitious use. Any resemblance to actual events or persons, whether living or dead, is completely coincidental.

CONTENTS

ACKNOWLEDGEMENTS

Where do you start when it comes time to thank those who truly deserve credit? The pages are not long enough for them all, but I must pay homage to my beautiful wife Roxanne. Thanks for letting me get lost in my story when I needed to. Thanks for not getting mad when I didn't answer a question or ignored a comment, all because I was too wrapped up in writing; for the long nights I sat up in bed with the soft light of my computer glowing; for listening to snippets and paragraphs, taken completely out of context, no less. It has to be tough being married to a man whose brain is always trying to come up with something new to say, whether it be writing a book or a song… thank you.

To my daughter Jordan, (my beautiful, creative, talented, incredibly photogenic daughter), you have never stopped amazing me. Thank you for the encouragement and support. You make being a *Daddy* awesome. Thank you for letting me bounce ideas off of you and for pointing me in all the right directions. You are the best!

To my parents, Phillip and Carolyn, I can't thank you enough for your unyielding support and belief in your oldest son. I am who I am because of you. You both make me proud and give me the courage to do what I do. I learned what I learned about this crazy world from living all over it; from Georgia to Australia to the Philippines and everywhere in between. What an amazing life I had growing up as your child. This book is for you.

To Travis, Sage, Cindy and Jennifer, thank you for reading both the short story and the novel before anyone else. Thanks for your honest criticism and encouragement and for being the guinea pigs. Somebody's got to do it. Without your help I would not have been able to present my story in the proper light. You guys rock!

To Jeb Blount, a successful and talented writer in his own right, thank you for taking the time out of your incredibly hectic schedule to read my story. Thank you for the insider details and suggestions. I owe you a round of golf buddy, but I will probably have to give you a ton of strokes these days.

We all have it hidden inside ourselves, a light that illuminates the possibilities. Listen close and follow that voice that tells you to climb the mountain. The one that says, "You only live once." Grab hold to the wind and go for your dream. The journey there is amazing.

This book has been a labor of love. I hope you enjoy reading it as much as I have writing it. God Bless,

Phillip *Derrick* Hampton

"Curiosity will conquer fear even more than bravery will."
- James Stephens

PROLOGUE

So Here She Lay

"Pardon me, boys, is that the Chattanooga Choo Choo..." It sounded almost like a dream, but she knew it was a nightmare. The tune brought her back to reality like smelling salts. How he got the radio to play that song was beyond her. The sweet and pungent stench of vomit and blood filled her nostrils. The bag over her face intensified the odor to the point where she could barely breathe. She wanted to scream, but the tall man had already punished her twice for doing just such a thing. So here she lay, hands tied together, head covered with a burlap bag, the locket her parents had given her on her birthday twisted around her neck. She was bouncing around like a rag doll in the backseat of the brand-new blue-and-white '56 Chevy. Like a scared, helpless rag doll.

She must have puked while she was unconscious, after he put the bag over her head. She didn't remember it, but when she came to, vomit covered her face and had already soiled the bag. She knew where the blood came from—the tall man had hit her so hard that her nose bled like a water fountain. Her front tooth had cracked in half, and her lip split open at least an inch. It's crazy how much blood comes from the nose and lips. It often looks like a gunshot wound. Her stomach was so sore, every bump the car made filled her with agonizing pain. She had had the wind knocked out of her one time before...cheerleading, when her spotter missed her on the way down from the top of the pyramid. But never had she been punched in the stomach, and definitely not by a grown man. It took so long for her air to come back that she thought she would die right then and there.

She had already given up hope on being rescued. She wasn't sure if it had been three days or three weeks, and until he put her in the car, she didn't even know if it was day or night. She knew it was night now because she could make out blurry images through the stitching in the burlap, and the sun definitely wasn't shining. Rain hit her skin when he walked her to the car, but it must have been a slow, soft rain because she couldn't hear it coming down.

At first she was angry. She threatened him. She told him how her daddy and brothers would cut him into pieces and feed him to the pigs. She warned him of the torture he would suffer at their hands, at God's hands. Then she begged. She cried like she had never cried. Pleaded for his sympathy. She would cry and ask, "Why?" She told him how she was a good person, how she went to church. How one time she saw a dog left for dead on the side of the road, all mangy and skinny, and how she picked him up in a blanket and nursed him back to health. How she named him Buddy and how he couldn't sleep without her there. Then she bargained. She told him her daddy had money and he would pay him anything he wanted. She said she wouldn't tell anybody, not her family, not the police. If he let her go, he would never have to worry because she was a woman of her word. She even offered to give him all of her. She tried to sound sexy and sensual. She was only fifteen years old and had never been with a boy, but she told him she could do everything he dreamed of, anything he wanted.

Nothing worked. He came into the dimly lit basement often. She figured it must have been every eight hours or so, but she couldn't be sure. The first two times, she screamed at him and cussed him for everything she had in her, and he beat her relentlessly with a leather strap, so she decided it would be best not to cause trouble anymore. She would sit on the musty cot with squeaky springs, one leg chained to it like a dog in the yard. Just enough slack to walk a couple of feet. She would sit there while he changed out her bedpan and brought her food and water. He would never talk, except to say, "Shh," which he did even after beating her. He would comb her hair and play old music from the big-band days. Then he would take out his pencils and paper and sketch her portrait, only to rip up the paper and storm out of the room. She heard "Chattanooga Choo Choo" so many times, she knew it by heart.

So here she lay, in the big backseat. She knew she should have never stuck her thumb out. She knew better. But it is truly frightening, the stubbornness of a teenager mad at her parents. They would not let her go to the campout, and why not? Simply because she was only fifteen. All of her friends were going, and she was a good girl. She studied hard, made good grades. There was no reason she shouldn't be able to go. That's why she climbed out of her window that night and started down the lonely highway, one and a half miles to the gas station where she would use a pay phone to call her best friend, Ellen, to come get her. Ellen turned sixteen a month earlier and had her license. Ellen offered to pick her up at her house, but she knew her daddy would hear Ellen coming down the deserted road like a deer hears a stepped-on twig. Forget about pulling into her yard. That was much too risky. Better to meet at the filling station. She could make it to the campout and be back before dawn, slip back into bed, and her folks would never know. Perfect plan…except she never realized how spooky that road was at night and how long a mile and a half is when you hear every hoot owl and windblown branch screaming at you like the bogeyman. She was actually relieved to see the headlights come over the hill. Just smile and ask for a quick ride to the station, easy peasy. The man had nice eyes and was dressed to the nines, very professional. He rolled down the window and was more than happy to oblige her request. She never would have thought the bogeyman drove a blue-and-white '56 Chevy.

So here she lay. Wondering how her parents would take the news that she was dead. How her brothers would handle school with the weight of what happened to her wearing on them. She even worried about Buddy and whether he would ever sleep again. She knew she was going to die. He didn't talk, but she could tell. In the last few days, she could feel that certainty closing in around her like a cold blanket. Still, he didn't have to hit her. She was being good. She never saw that one coming. One minute he was setting down her food, the next he was pounding her in the stomach and the face and then covering her head with a burlap sack. The last thing she remembered before the radio brought her back to consciousness was the wetness on her skin from the rain and the sound of the engine as he turned the ignition.

When the car finally stopped moving, she could hear the water rushing. She wondered if it was the Cottonwood River. She loved that river so much. Her family would picnic on its banks in the summer. Her daddy would play his guitar and they would sing along. She guessed if she had to die, there wasn't a prettier place. It's funny how the mind rationalizes things. She wished she had kissed Tony Faust. He was going to be at that stupid campout, and she had had a crush on him since the ninth grade. She and Ellen giggled as they talked about how she was going to kiss him that night. She even practiced on herself in the mirror. "Just enough tongue to make it sexy but not so much to make you a whore," Ellen told her. She wondered what her funeral would be like, who would be there. What would her tombstone say? *Here Lies Abigail Lowery. Loved, Lost, but Not Forgotten.*

The door swung open, and he grabbed her by her hair through the bag. She screamed, but this time he didn't hit her; he just kept dragging her along the ground. When he finally let her go, she was sobbing, quietly reciting the Lord's Prayer. She was grateful her mother taught it to her all those years ago.

"Deliver us from evil…" *God must be busy,* she thought. At that moment, the tall man finally spoke to her.

"This is my mother's fault," he said. "I told her I couldn't draw the faces right, but she kept making me draw, over and over and over again. I told her, 'Mother, I don't like drawing,' but the bitch watched me like the devil. 'Leonard, you will never amount to anything.…Leonard, you are a moron....Leonard, you disappoint me.' Are you happy now, Mother?" he screamed into the rain, which had picked up its pace dramatically.

Abigail was on her knees, head bowed and still covered in burlap, praying relentlessly, when she felt the tall man grab her hair through the sack and jerk her head backward. She felt the cold, searing pain jolt through her neck like electricity and fire mixed together. Her throat filling with blood, she could hear the prayer only in her mind now. Syrupy blood replaced the oxygen in her lungs. She gargled and gasped for air, but none was available for her on this night. She toppled forward and lay motionless on the wet grass, hands still tied together, eyes wide open as he pulled the bag off of her head. She was amazingly grateful in that last second of her life. She watched the Cottonwood River rush by as she faded into that long, lost memory. So here she lay, Abigail Lowery. Loved, Lost, but Not Forgotten.

WHITE LINES

The white lines flew by like long, skinny darts in the night. Thaddeus Taylor had been driving nonstop since he left Washington, DC, nearly six hours earlier. The "E" was warning him of the very real possibility of running out of gas.

"I need a break anyway," he mumbled to himself.

He pulled his Lincoln Navigator off of I-70 at the first station he saw. Somewhere about fifty miles from Pittsburgh, around 10:30 at night, he found his oasis. The orange, red, and green of a 7-Eleven looks like home when you're road weary. Leaning against the car, he pulled out his cell phone and typed M-O-M. The phone made its usual noises. He probably couldn't tell you anybody's number, but as long as he could spell their names, then he could call them. He found himself thinking how he used to know every one of his friends' phone numbers. Hell, he could still remember Paul Rose's home number after all these years...620-340-1331. Nowadays if you weren't a name on his contact list, chances were that he wouldn't call you. Not because he was arrogant or rude; it was a simple matter of not knowing the number.

"Hello?" the voice answered in a somewhat sleepy, somewhat worried tone.

"Hi, Mom. I'm filling up somewhere in Pennsylvania. I just wanted to let you know I'm all right."

"Thank you, sweetheart," she said. "Thad, why don't you stop for the night? Check into a motel there and get some rest. The funeral isn't for two days."

Removing the cap to the gas tank, he answered, "Naw, I'm ok, Mom. I'm gonna grab a cup of coffee and get some more miles in. How are Linda and the kids holding up?"

Linda and Paul Rose had the kind of marriage that has become a rare commodity these days: "till death do us part." They had three kids, the oldest out of college, the middle in high school, and the youngest about to start kindergarten. The youngest, like the first, wasn't planned, but his dad spoiled him rotten. Paul had met Linda when her family moved to town the last year of high school. She didn't know a soul and was shy and mad as hell that her daddy brought her to this little "hick town" named Emporia. But then she met Paul, and this little "hick town" didn't seem so bad after all. She loved his strong physique and brooding good looks. At six foot four, he was the tallest kid in school. He had sandy-blond hair, blue eyes, and a beautiful smile. That smile…there was something about that smile that Linda couldn't resist. And he laughed all the time, which made her laugh, which made every day in her new town feel more like home.

It was a brief courtship to say the least. She was swept off her feet not long after meeting him, and by the time prom rolled around, the two were rarely seen apart. She loved his friends, especially Thad. She reckoned if Paul Rose loved him, then she loved him, too. They would all double date, goof off together, just normal high school teenager stuff. One time they all went down to the Cottonwood River, camped out, and told stories. She learned a lot about her husband-to-be that night, why he believed what he believed, why he was who he was.

She was three months along by the time they graduated from high school. Her parents were devastated, but not Linda. She didn't plan it, but she loved Paul Rose more than anything, and although a baby rushed things, their marriage was inevitable. There was no way she was letting him go, anyway. He was the perfect man. The perfect big, kindhearted, handsome, funny, devoted man. They were married not long after high school, and after the baby came, her parents lost their devastation. In fact, they replaced it with newfound jubilation. Babies have a way of doing that. Linda's world was perfect.

Funny how life throws you curveballs. One minute your husband is driving home from working at the meat factory, just as he had since before you were married; the next minute his Honda Accord is hit head-on by a drunk driver who crossed the median in a pickup truck on I-35. Why is it the drunk one always seems to walk away from the wreckage and the sober one draws his last breath at the scene?

"Linda seems to be all right, but honestly I think it's just the shock of the whole thing and the business of planning a funeral. Something tells me after everyone goes home and things slow down, she will have a tough time," his mother said.

"I know, Mom," Thad said, contemplating that thought. "Let me finish gassing up. I'll see you in the morning. Try to get some sleep."

"Be careful, honey," she said. "I don't want to plan your funeral."

"I will, Mom. I love you. See you soon."

Thad put the phone in his pocket and the nozzle back into the pump. He headed inside and found the hot coffee. One cup, two Slim Jims, and $75.63 later, he was back on the long road to Emporia, Kansas. Headed to bury his best friend, Paul Rose. They all called him Rosie.

Rosie was always bigger than his classmates. Even in the first-grade school pictures, he was the tall kid in the photo. He had "street smarts," as he liked to say. No better than a C-plus student in school, he was a genius at dealing with people and getting what he wanted.

One time he conned a dry cleaner out of twenty dollars for an imaginary school fund-raiser, using nothing but a smile and his words. The "Three Amigos," as Rosie, Thad, and their little buddy, Marcus Pawley, used to call themselves, quickly spent the booty between the arcade and one issue of *Playboy* magazine that Rosie purchased for them. He could get away with that sort of stuff because of his size, and Thad and Marcus loved it.

Rosie had a relatively normal upbringing. A devoted father and a caring mother were a constant in his life. He was an only child, though not by design. His was a difficult birth, and afterward his mother was unable to have children. Not having a sibling was a double-edged sword for Rosie. On the one hand, he had it pretty good for a middle-class kid. His parents could provide things for him that they wouldn't be able to if he had a brother or sister, such as nice vacations, all the cool toys, even his own television set for his bedroom. On the other hand, it left him craving companionship.

With no one around near his age to share things with, friendship was a premium to Rosie. That's probably why Thad was so important to him. Thad was also an only child. They had a bond that went deep. They were assigned seats next to each other in the first grade, and from that day on they were pretty much inseparable. Nearly every weekend, and definitely every summer, Thad and Rosie hung out. They lived on the same street and rode their bikes to each other's houses. Rosie's dad jokingly called their street "Rose Taylor Road." He said the city should put in a bike lane just for them because they used the street more than the cars did. In the fourth grade, they met Marcus, and the Three Amigos were born. Emporia was never going to be the same.

Rosie's great-grandparents were Irish immigrants who made their way to Kansas along with an influx of thousands of other Irishmen in the late 1800s. They were looking for that dream of hope and prosperity that America so willingly offered, and a pamphlet titled *The State of Kansas and Irish Immigration*, written by an Irish reverend named

Thomas Butler, provided just the encouragement they needed to cross the pond in search of a new life.

Hard work was almost a genetic lineage in the Rose family. Rosie's great-grandfather worked for a lumberyard in Leavenworth, Kansas, until he died of a heart attack on the job. His grandfather went to work for the railroad at the age of sixteen, until the army drafted him in World War II. Storming the beach at Normandy, he lost his right leg and nearly died. After he healed, he went back to work for the railroad. He said, "God saw fit to give me two legs in case I lost one." He was given a pension and a gold watch on his retirement. He passed away two weeks later. Rosie's dad said that it was because without his work, Rosie's grandfather didn't feel he was worth anything. His father went to work at the slaughterhouse in Emporia just out of high school and stayed there until his retirement forty years later.

As for Rosie, the apple fell next to the tree. He didn't know the word *lazy*, and his size implied that he could work like a mule. Big guys seem to have more expected of them in that department. His dad got him a job at the slaughterhouse when he was eighteen, and he had been there ever since. Working his way up from grunt to floor supervisor. He was appreciative of his position and tried to be a good boss. He took it hard one year when he had to let half of his employees go. Corporate made the rules and he followed; he just felt responsible. He was a big man with a big heart.

"Damn, Rosie," Thad said to no one.

Thad drove on into the darkness, satellite radio tuned into the '70s station. "That's the Way I Like It" by KC and the Sunshine Band belted out its rhythmic beat as he heard the cement joints clicking underneath his tires at a steady seventy-five miles per hour. White lines mesmerizing him like a Vegas magician. His mind drifted back in time, back to his youth.

TREE HOUSE

It was a hot day in Emporia, Kansas, but it was a good one. 1975 had been a wet year but at least the rain from the previous week had finally subsided. The sky was blue and the grass was green. The Cottonwood River was full and fast, very fast.

"Marcus, let me have some," Rosie ordered. "You're gonna smoke the whole thing."

Sitting in the tree house that his older brother Tommy had helped him build, Marcus Pawley took a deep, long drag on the Marlboro Red that he'd stolen from his dad's pack. He blew the smoke out in a feeble attempt to make a ring, but he was able to muster up only a flimsy white cloud and a hacking cough. His plain, white, long-sleeved T-shirt and hand-me-down bargain-bin jeans complemented his army-style black-rimmed glasses. His hair always seemed to be slightly sloppy, kind of like a wet puppy…cute, but you wouldn't really want to touch it.

"Don't be so whiny. Here, go crazy." Marcus choked the words out as he handed Rosie the ash-tipped paper.

The radio cranked "Kung Fu Fighting" by Carl Douglas, and Marcus did his best karate moves as Rosie took the cigarette from his "ninja" hand.

Wearing a blue-and-white, horizontally striped shirt and faded jeans with holes in the knees, Thad leaned over the edge, trying to take a picture of the old tree trunk holding up their summer retreat. Through his lens, it looked a mile long, distorted, and interesting. That's what he loved about pictures, and that's what made him a camera geek. The ability to take an everyday object and turn it into something special fascinated him. It was not uncommon to find him with his Minolta camera hanging around his neck; in fact, it was unusual to find him without it.

Thad's grandfather was a combat correspondent for the marines. After World War II, he freelanced for magazines such as *Life* and *Time*. Traveling the globe as he plied his trade, he built a reputation as a solid photographer, a go-to guy for the tough shots. Thad idolized him. When his grandfather died, he left his favorite Minolta to his only grandson, and Thad had a natural eye for it.

"Anybody can take a picture," his grandfather would tell him, "but not everybody can capture a real moment in time."

In his Kansas City Chiefs football jersey and Levi's 501s, Rosie spoke up. "Guys, look at these hooters," he said, holding the current issue of *Playboy* sideways with the cig hanging out of his mouth like a gangster from an old-timey movie. "Miss June 1975." Taking the smoke from his mouth, Rosie let a slow wolf whistle slide off his lips..

Thad and Marcus took a long look at the picture. The silence was a dead giveaway that the fourteen-year-old boys were awestruck.

"Last time I saw boobs like that, I was kissing Thad's mom good night," Marcus said, causing Rosie to bust out laughing and Thad to frog Marcus's arm.

"Knock it off, Marcus, before I knock you out," Thad said, giving Marcus a look like he meant it. Still, he couldn't help but smile a little.

"I'd like to see Allie Thompson's ta-tas," Rosie said, staring intently at the naked girl. "Did you guys see her in that T-shirt the other day? She's got the tits of a senior!" Rosie always cut to the chase.

Marcus chimed in. "Oh, man, I bet she's been wearing a bra for like a year."

"Guys, come on," Thad said, ever the gentleman. "That's not cool."

"We know you like her, Thad," Rosie said in a mocking tone.

"Yeah, we might have to make an exception," Marcus added, "and let a girl join our tree house. Thad and Allie sittin' in a tree…"

Marcus and Rosie laughed, Rosie rubbing Thad's hair like a puppy.

"Cut it out," Thad warned them both.

"Relax, man," Rosie said. "We're just messing with ya."

Quickly trying to change the subject, Thad let out an exaggerated sigh. "Man, I'm bored. We've been out of school for over a month. By the time Labor Day rolls around, I'm gonna lose my mind."

"Are you saying you would rather be back in school?" Marcus asked.

"Man you're crazy if you think summer is too long," Rosie said with wonderment.

"No, I don't wanna go back to school. I'm just saying there's gotta be something else to do besides sit in a tree all day and steal Marcus's dad's smokes," Thad said.

"Like what?" Marcus asked.

"We could go to the junkyard and snoop around for some cool stuff," Rosie said.

"Better not, man," Marcus warned. "Trash-Man Willie's got a junkyard dog now. I heard he attacked two kids there the other day who were snooping around. Bit one of their toes clean off."

Thad and Rosie shook their head "no," as if to say *never mind*.

"We can go to the ball field and see what losers are playing today," Marcus said.

Rosie answered, "No, they wrapped up the season two weeks ago. They ain't playing any more games this summer."

The boys sat around the tree house contemplating just what they could get into. Thad looked around the wooden structure. It was surprisingly well built, especially considering it was made of scrap lumber and odd parts, mostly stolen from Trash-Man Willie's pre-junkyard-dog days. There was a sturdy ladder attached to the tree trunk that allowed a quick entrance and a pole at the back that allowed for an even quicker exit. A window was cut out on each side, which allowed easy viewing of possible trespassers as well as a nice breeze to blow through, keeping it decently cool even in the hot Kansas summer. Fittingly, there was a Kiss *Hotter Than Hell* poster on the wall. Tommy and Marcus had built a bench seat on one wall that opened to store the tree house essentials, such as flashlights, matches, girly magazines, plastic forks, Coca-Colas, canned fruit, and one rusty, old can opener.

"All the comforts of home," Marcus told Thad and Rosie when he first introduced them to his sanctuary among the branches. The tree house was back in the woods on Marcus's uncle's property, and Marcus loved escaping there to get away from his uncomfortable life.

No one had said anything for at least a minute while the boys continued to rack their brains for something fun to do. Then Thad had an idea.

"How 'bout heading down to the Cottonwood and hang out? We could fix up that old tire swing or something."

Thad knew it when he said it: Marcus's older brother Tommy had hung that *old* tire swing down by the Cottonwood River.

"Sorry, Marcus," Thad said respectfully. "I wasn't thinking."

"Naw, that's ok, Thad," Marcus replied. "We can go down there."

HOWARD JOHNSON AND F4S

The truck went around Thad's Lincoln Navigator with a loud bellow of its horn, snapping him back to the present. It was 2:30 in the morning, but that was 3:30 back in DC, and he needed more gas and a break. Thad pointed the car toward the next exit.

He pulled into the quick stop and got out of the car. It reminded him of a scene from a cheesy movie. The sound of eighteen-wheelers could be heard rolling by on the interstate. The speakers overhead played peppy music alternating with a man's voice encouraging you to relieve yourself of your money in their place of business. "Don't forget to get a thirty-two-ounce drink before you get back on the road," the friendly voice said.

Selecting regular unleaded and leaving the nozzle in the gas tank, Thad headed inside the convenience store, bathroom on the right and coffee on the left. Due to the lateness of the hour and the heaviness of his eyelids, Thad decided to entertain the bathroom and bypass the coffee. The mirror in the bathroom showed the tiredness in his dark brown eyes. His black, cropped hair needed attention, and the bags under his eyes were turning blue from sleep deprivation. Even still, Thaddeus Taylor was a handsome man. He had a baby face that still got him carded from time to time. He used to get mad and think, *Card me? Jesus, I just got back from Afghanistan.* But now it was more like, *Awesome, they want my ID for a drink. I still got it.* He stood six foot on the nose and kept himself in shape; he ran, worked out, and rock climbed.

He splashed some water on his face. With both hands propping him up against the sink, he stared deep into his own dark eyes and decided it was time to call it quits for the evening. Not even a thirty-two-ounce Mountain Dew would keep his eyes open for much longer this time. There was a Howard Johnson across the street, and the thought of sleep sounded too good to pass up. Back outside, he returned the nozzle to its proper position in the gas pump and climbed back into the car, thinking of Marcus, of what he went through as a child.

Marcus was a good kid, a good kid with a rough life. His father was an alcoholic widower who liked to use Marcus as a punching bag, especially when he was drunk, and he was drunk most of the time. Marcus was prone to wearing long-sleeved shirts in the summer to cover the marks left by his dad's temper. He would always play off the bruises with a joke or a funny excuse. He had the inordinate ability to be funny as hell at the completely inappropriate time.

One of the few things in Marcus's life that was dependable was his big brother, Tommy. Tommy was the one who would fend off their dad when he was violent. He was ferociously protective of his little brother, Marcus. He once pounded three kids for picking on Marcus while riding the school bus. Tommy got off with two days' suspension from the principal. The other kids weren't so lucky. They all got off with black eyes, a few missing front teeth, and one got a forever-crooked broken nose.

On June 8, 1974, at 6:00 p.m., an F4 tornado ripped through the city of Emporia, killing six and injuring hundreds. It laid waste to buildings, homes, trailers, farms…and tire swings. Everyone in the town was affected in one way or another, especially Marcus.

On June 8, 1974, at 7:52 p.m., they found Tommy's body in a trailer park. He was visiting his girlfriend when the tornado hit. Every trailer was destroyed, and although most people survived, Tommy was not as fortunate. A two-by-four hit his head so hard, it cracked his skull open like an egg.

After that, Marcus's dad went from bad to worse. Sometimes Marcus would have bruises so big on his back and legs, it looked like he had a run-in with a bulldozer. But Marcus always made jokes. In retrospect Thad was sure it was to cover the emotional scars, a coping mechanism to just plain survive the situation God had seen fit to put him in.

The Three Amigos was a salvation for Marcus. Thad and Rosie accepted him quickly into their clique. If it wasn't for his buddies when he lost Tommy, Marcus was sure he wouldn't have made it. He clung to their friendship like a vine to an oak. He knew he was the runt and the guy to most likely get frogged the hardest, but he didn't care. Thad and Rosie were as close to blood as he could get, and they treated him with mutual respect. So Marcus endured. Life is a bitch and hope springs eternal—two clichés that summed up Marcus's childhood.

But after all this time, after everything he went through, Marcus had done ok for himself. He learned the pawnshop business from his uncle Mike and had opened up a store in downtown Emporia, Pawley's Pawn and Purchase. Thad always thought it had a nice ring to it. Marcus had a two-bedroom, two-bath home about six miles out of town. Divorced, no kids, he had the same mutt, Scrappy, for the last eighteen years. Still, he had his own business, no debt, and peace of mind knowing that he made it through his hellish childhood with most of his sense intact. Not bad, all things considered.

Pulling into the HoJo parking lot, Thad grabbed his duffel bag and made his way to the front desk. He took the last room available, threw his bag on the floor, kicked off his shoes, and collapsed on the bed. Not even taking time to remove his clothes, he quickly gave in to that comforting invitation we call sleep, thinking of Marcus, and Rosie, and Allie Thompson…and poor Tommy.

TRAVELING PHOTOGRAPHERS

After a measly four hours' sleep, Thad was up early the next morning. A quick cup of coffee and a free continental breakfast in the hotel lobby, and he was on the road again. With good traffic he figured he would make it to Emporia by two o'clock. He spoke briefly to his mother and then put the SUV in drive. Next was a call to his office in DC.

"Hi, Marge," he said. "I need you to let Ken know I will have those shots from Syria ready by next week."

Marge was Ken's secretary and Ken was Ken Waller, the senior photo editor for *National Geographic* magazine or NGM as they liked to call themselves these days. Thad always thought *National Geographic* magazine was classier, but what did he know? He was a staff photographer for the rag and busy as hell. He had his laptop with him and planned on getting some editing time in when he got to Emporia, but he needed his boss to know that he could still get the job done even though he was burying his best friend back home. The news never waited, after all, and the one thing that set NGM apart from its competition was its photos. Anyway, Thad had no choice. *One day,* he thought, *I'm gonna pack it all in and slow down.*

Thad had a knack for getting the right shots at the right time. Once, on assignment in Mexico, he was documenting the plight of small town families whose lives were being destroyed by the drug cartels. He had pictures of faces and homes, of goats and bicycles, of old Chevy trucks and farms. But the one he still remembers, the one he can't erase from his mind, is the photograph of a man's head on a stake in the town square, his young son and wife crying at the foot of the post. Apparently he had said no to the cartel when they asked him to run drugs. *Asked* was a gentle word; *told* was more like it. He was a principled man, a religious man, a family man…a dead man. That image got him a raise at the magazine. That image got him a year of therapy with a psychologist.

Like his grandfather, Thad went into the bad places, the harsh places. Early on, he was the first one to volunteer. Later on, he was the first one chosen. "A traveling photographer's life is a lonely life," his grandfather used to tell him. How true it rang these days. The closest thing he'd had to an intimate relationship lately was with his laptop computer; he was 'intimately' familiar with its photo-editing software.

Still though, Thad loved the art of photography. The ability to create something out of thin air. The business of photography, you could keep. He was weary of the travel, the long nights, the broken relationships. Sometimes you are given a gift. What you do with that gift is your choosing. Thad chose to photograph the world and the people that lived in it…really 'lived' in it. What it cost him was the ability to really live in his.

He was an award-winning photographer. Actually, he was a multiple award-wining photographer. He won a National Press Photographers Award and an Oskar Barnack Award. He was even a finalist for the World Press Photo of the Year…twice. He had definitely built a distinguished career for himself.

From his grandfather to his high school counselor, everyone knew Thad would be a photographer. Some kids pick up fads, some pick up professions. He had always said, ever since he was a little boy, that he was going to take pictures just like his granddad. As time went on and he got older, he started to realize that he could be just like his grandfather. If he wanted to be a professional photographer, all he had to do was work hard, study, and go for it. His counselor recommended journalism for his higher studies. It was a perfect fit. Journalism put him in the middle of the current issues, and photography captured what he wanted to say about it. They say a picture is worth a thousand words; Thad reckoned it was worth a thousand journalists.

To tell a story with a photograph is a talent that few possess. You have to be able to convey the visceral emotion that is present in that moment to someone sipping his latte at a Starbucks five thousand miles away. You have to make a grown man, reading the morning news in New York, tear up over his eggs and bacon at a child holding the hand of his dead mother after a tsunami in Thailand. With that one picture, the man in New York knows the gut-wrenching heartache and overwhelming catastrophe that the child was going through, without even reading one word. And Thad could do it, better than most, perhaps better than anyone.

If indeed he did pack it all in, it wouldn't be an easy thing. What would he do? Where would he go? How do you take a life and turn it into a new life but still be happy and enjoy what you're doing? That's the million-dollar question.

Thad was letting those questions run through his mind like a kaleidoscope when he heard the loud bang. The car jerked hard to the left, but he was able to get it under control. He slowed the vehicle down and could feel the unmistakable thump of a flat tire. He pulled into the emergency lane and got out.

"Damn it," Thad said kneeling beside the blown tire. He opened the back door to the SUV and found his jack and spare. Turning the lug nuts and cussing the Ford service department for tightening them too damn much, he eventually got the wheel off and replaced it with his spare. At least he had a full-use spare, not one of those "don't drive over 50 mph or over one hundred miles" type of doughnut spare.

Throwing the blown tire into the back of the SUV, he paused momentarily before closing the door. It reminded him of the old tire swing they hung all those years ago down by the Cottonwood River...

TIRE SWING

The Cottonwood River wound and bent through the land just south of Emporia, flowing eastward until it joined up with the Neosho River. In Emporia, it touched the south end of Peter Pan Park, moving its liquid contents through miles of twists and turns. The week before had brought torrential rains, and the old river was churning. Thad was taking pictures of the angry waterway while Rosie and Marcus were trying to scare the hell out of ducks, running them back into the park. The waterfowl were squawking like busted accordions. Looking at them, Thad smiled and snapped off a couple shots of his goofball buddies chasing mallards.

"Come on, guys," Thad said over the screaming birds, "let's get going. The tire swing ain't gonna fix itself."

Thad snapped one more shot and then began following the river's edge eastward out of the park. Rosie and Marcus fell in behind him like good soldiers.

"Hey, Thad," Marcus said. "Why does a chicken coop have two doors? Because if it had four, it would be a sedan."

"Ha ha ha," Thad said.

But then a little chuckle started in Thad's throat. Rosie followed suit. Although they both knew the joke was lame, they couldn't help but snicker even more. Before long, all three boys were laughing hard.

"That's the stupidest joke I've ever heard," Rosie said through his cackling.

"That's…why…it's…so…funny," Thad said, trying to get the words out.

It took a few minutes for the laughter to calm as the boys trudged onward. They cut across a large open field to save some time, catching back up to the river on the other side of the clearing. From there they followed its bank until they reached Soden Dam. A few skipped rocks and broken sticks thrown over the watery precipice, and they were on their way again. It was a decent walk to the spot where Tommy had built the swing, down past the water treatment plant, a couple of miles out of town. Time moved by like frozen syrup, so Rosie started humming. The hum eventually boiled over into a full-fledged tune. "Here she comes just a-walking down the street…"

The other two followed in time. "Do wa diddy diddy dum diddy do…"

The familiar song kept the boys occupied until they reached a stream that emptied into the Cottonwood. The kids liked to call it "Crap Creek" because of its proximity to the water treatment plant. A few years before, Marcus's brother, Tommy, and a couple of his friends had built a rickety bridge out of old one-by-tens and two-by-fours they had scrounged from Willie's junkyard. Problem was, Thad, Rosie, and Marcus were standing at the very spot where the bridge was supposed to be, but it wasn't there. The creek was too wide to jump and the water was a little too deep to cross.

"Where the hell's the bridge?" Marcus asked, scratching his head.

"We are in the right place, aren't we?" Rosie asked, also scratching his head.

"This is the right place," Thad answered. "Tornado must've taken it."

"Reckon that's at least six feet deep," Rosie said, looking at the water as the three boys tried to figure a way across. "Personally, I don't want to wade it."

The small creek was also swollen from the days of rain that had inundated the area.

"Me neither," Marcus said.

"There's got to be some way to get across," Thad said, looking up and down the creek bank for a solution.

About one hundred feet away, Thad saw the answer to their problem. A small pine tree had fallen and lay perfectly across the creek. It did not have any branches on it, so Thad guessed it was a dead tree that the storm blew over easily, like a folded beach umbrella in an ocean gale.

"Hey, guys, check it out," Thad said, pointing to the fallen timber.

All three boys stood at the foot of the makeshift bridge, each waiting for another to cross first.

"I don't know," Thad said. "It doesn't look sturdy to me."

"Looks slippery, too," Rosie added.

"I didn't know my best friends were girls," Marcus said as he jumped up on the log. "I'll go first, you chickens."

Marcus placed his right foot on the old pine and stomped it hard enough to shake the tree. "Seems ok to me," he said.

Bringing his other foot up to join in the march, Marcus slowly shuffled his way across. Halfway to the other side, his left foot slipped. He threw his hands out like a circus high-wire performer and regained his balance. "Careful right here, guys," he said. "It's slipperier than a frog in an oil pan." He made his way to the opposing side and watched as Rosie began to follow suit. Rosie moved twice as slow as Marcus, but then again he was twice as big. The tree groaned with each step, as if to say, "Get off!," but Rosie, too, reached the bank, with Thad following right behind him.

"Easy peasy lemon squeezy," Marcus said with a grin.

The boys continued on their journey. After a brief stint through a heavily wooded area, they came upon a small clearing, and they knew they had reached their destination. There, lying on the ground by the Cottonwood River, was an old tire with a rope still tied to it. The tree was missing several of its larger branches but had survived the tornado from the previous year mostly intact. A path was clearly marked through the woods where the twister had danced among the trees like a bowling ball in a dynamite factory. Looking up at the grand old oak, Thad figured one of the branches still hanging out over the river was sturdy enough for the job.

"What about that one?" Thad asked, pointing to the limb.

Rosie answered, "Yes sir. That one oughta do it. Give me the rope, and I'll climb up there."

"No way, man," Marcus blurted out. "It was my brother who made this swing, and I'm gonna be the one to fix it. I'm climbing up. Give me a boost."

Rosie and Thad looked at each other and then back at their determined yet small friend.

"Ok, Marcus. Just be careful," Thad said.

Marcus tied one end of the rope to his belt. Rosie and Thad stood next to the tree and cupped their hands together to give Marcus a firm stepping-stone. Marcus put one leg in their hands and sprang upward just high enough to grab the lowest limb. Thad and Rosie were well aware of Marcus's tendency to prove himself, especially after Tommy died, but they also knew that if he hurt himself, his dad would hurt him even more. He worked his leg onto the limb and then stood upright. Looking up at the next limb, Marcus started singing, "Spider man, spider man..." And then he jumped straight up and grabbed hold of the next limb.

"Careful, man," Rosie called out.

Swinging back and forth like he was playing on the monkey bars, Marcus made chimp noises.

"Cut it out, dude," Thad said.

Laughing at his friends, Marcus replied, "Quit worrying. You *are* a bunch of little g—Whoa!"

Of course Marcus's one-handed monkey grip slipped loose from the branch. He dropped straight down. Luckily or unluckily, however you want to look at it, the previous branch stopped his fall. He landed on it full straddle, the wood slamming hard into his groin. Marcus let out a short but high-pitched whimper. He was able to get both hands on the limb to steady himself or he would have rolled over, in super slow motion, down to the ground.

Both Thad and Rosie instinctively grabbed their crotches.

Thad looked shocked. "Marcus, are you ok?"

Rosie looked shocked. "Dude, that had to hurt!"

Marcus looked shocked. "—girls."

Marcus just sat there straddling the branch, frozen like a squirrel hiding from its prey, "Ohhhh, my balls...I'm never gonna have kids."

Both the boys on the ground started laughing hysterically.

"Don't worry, Marcus," Rosie said through his laughter, "it ain't like you were ever gonna use them anyway!"

Thad and Rosie took several minutes before they could contain themselves, which was fine with Marcus. It took him several minutes before he could move.

After the laughter from the ground level subsided, Marcus very gingerly made his way back up the tree. Once he reached his target, he untied the rope from his belt. Throwing it around the limb, he pulled until the tire was high enough off the ground to provide some good swing room. Then he tied the rope good and tight to the limb.

As he turned to make his way back down, he noticed something at the water's edge, near the bank. He couldn't make out what it was, but it was reflecting the sun's glare like a dull mirror.

"Hey, you guys see that?" he asked.

"See what?" Thad asked.

"That shiny thing in the water by the bank. What is that?"

Rosie made his way to the edge and peered into the water. "What? I don't see nothing."

"To your right," Marcus answered.

Looking to his right, Rosie saw the object. It was caught on a branch that had fallen into the water, probably from the tornado. He bent over, stretching his long arm as far has he could, barely able to get one finger on it. As he pulled the trinket in, it slipped loose. Feeling as if he had just lost the Hope Diamond, he stabbed at the water as fast as he could. He just barely caught hold of the object by what felt like a thin cord. Lifting it out of the water, he saw it was a pendant on a silver chain.

"Check it out," he said.

Moving back down the tree, this time with newfound respect, Marcus made his way to the bottom.

The three boys stared at the jewelry.

"How old is it?" Marcus asked in bewilderment.

"I don't know," Thad answered. "I wonder who it belongs to."

Rosie felt a small catch on the side of the pendant and pressed. To their surprise the locket opened. The inside was full of muck, as if it had been in the water a long time. Rosie cleaned out the mud using the hem of his jersey. There was an inscription: *To Abigail. Love, Mom and Dad.*

PAWNSHOPS, KISSES, AND LIBRARIES

Swinging out over the water, the boys took turns trying out the revamped tire and rope.

"This tire swing is awesome," Rosie said, stretching the rope as high as he could get it with every swing.

"Be careful, man," Thad warned, "don't fall into the river. It's too dangerous right now."

"Duh," Rosie replied, swinging even higher than before.

"Why don't we take the necklace down to my uncle's pawn shop and see how much money we can get for it?" Marcus asked out of the blue.

That caught the other two boys' attention. They decided they had had enough of the tire swing; it was time to go collect some cash. Rosie led the way as the three young men tore through woods, heading back to town. Over the fallen tree, past Crap Creek, through Peter Pan Park and into the heart of Emporia. Excited by the prospect of pawned riches, they barely slowed their pace. Running hard the final stint and almost out of breath, they turned the corner by the hardware store only slowing down when they reached Emporia Pawn. Taking just a second to catch their wind, they burst through the door.

"Marcus?" Marcus's uncle asked in a surprised tone.

"Hey, Uncle Mike." Marcus panted. "We found a cool piece of jewelry...and wanted to know...if you might want to buy it."

Mike Shaw grew up in Emporia. The oldest brother to Marcus's mom, he was as close to his nephew as he could be, taking into account the fact that Marcus's dad was a constant barrier. He knew Marcus had a tough life, losing his mother and brother and living with a hard man like his father. Mike would let Marcus work around the shop whenever he could, giving him some pocket change and the occasional odd item he couldn't sell.

"Jewelry, huh?" Uncle Mike asked. "Let me see what you got there."

He took the necklace from Thad and eyed it carefully. Opening the locket he read the inscription. "Where did you boys get this?"

"In the river, down by the tire swing," Rosie answered.

Uncle Mike continued studying the piece, "This style pendant is old, from the late '40s or '50s."

"Wow, that's like dinosaur old," Marcus exclaimed. "I bet it's worth a fortune!"

"How much?" Thad and Rosie asked at the same time.

Uncle Mike chuckled. "Slow down, fellows. It's not worth too much, but that inscription..." His words trailed off.

The boys stood there staring at him. Rosie finally said, "What?"

Uncle Mike put the necklace on the counter. "When I was a boy, around 1956, '57, there was a young girl...went missing. Just disappeared one night into thin air. The police looked for her. Her family looked for her. Hell, the whole town looked for her, but she was never found. Her name was Abigail Lowery. Years later they caught some psycho creep who'd kidnapped several girls and…well, let's just say the girls never made it home. They called him the Cottonwood Killer 'cause he'd dump their bodies in the river. I think they found nine girls in all but never found Abigail. He never confessed to it, but the cops were sure he was probably involved. Where'd you say you found this?"

Marcus answered, "Well, see, I was climbing a tree trying to fix Tommy's tire swing—the tornado ripped it down last year—anyway, Thad said he was bored from hanging out in the tree house and that we should fix the tire swing, so we went—"

"I don't need all the details, Marcus," Uncle Mike interrupted in a parental but gentle tone.

"Ok, sorry," Marcus said, "anyway, we saw it caught on a branch in the river. Rosie pulled it out and cleaned it up. We thought we could get something for it."

Studying it one last time, Uncle Mike handed the necklace back to Thad and said, "Aww…it's probably nothing anyways. Seriously, though boys, I can't give you anything for it. It just wouldn't sell with somebody else's name on it."

"Damn it," Rosie said, "uh, I mean, thanks anyway, sir."

With that, the boys left the pawn shop and headed down the street, kicking any unlucky piece of trash they happened upon like professional soccer players.

After a bit Thad spoke up. "Do you guys think this necklace is tied into that missing girl, Abigail Lowery?" Without waiting for an answer, he continued, "Why don't we go to the library and look at microfiche?"

"Micro Fish?" Rosie asked, very confused. "Why do we want to look at tiny little fish?"

Marcus stopped kicking the soda can he had corralled and stared at Rosie momentarily and then burst out laughing, "Micro*fiche,* not micro*fish,* knucklehead."

A good punch in the arm from Rosie stopped the merriment.

Thad laughed a little. Turning around so he could see Rosie, he said, "You know, the little films that look like tiny versions of X-rays the dentist takes. They have all the old newspapers on them and stuff. You put them in a projector, and it blows 'em up big enough so you can see 'em."

"I knew that," Rosie said in a suspiciously emphatic tone.

Nobody replied.

Thad noticed a sly grin developing on his friends' faces. Just then he felt a small tap on his right shoulder. It startled him just enough to jerk. He turned around to see who was causing the distraction, only to be standing face-to-face with Allie Thompson. Next to her was her best friend, Katey Jo McAnally.

Allie's blond hair was pulled back in a ponytail. She wore a dark blue, short-sleeved cotton shirt with a pale blue, knee-length skirt. She even had blue-and-white-checked clogs to complete her look. She always dressed well.

She had turned fourteen two weeks earlier, and her folks threw her a big party. Thad spent the whole time at the party trying to find the right thing to say and the right place to hide when she came his way. It was a fruitless practice in contradictions. The night ended with just a "Happy Birthday" and a "good night," but still Allie gave him the biggest smile of the evening and he imagined kissing her more than once.

"What'cha doing?" Allie asked Thad with an innocent grin.

"Micro*fishing* the library…I mean a pendant…Uh…it's a necklace…" Thad rambled with a peculiar smile.

Rosie and Marcus looked at each other and back at Thad.

Katey Jo said, "Do you mean micro*fiche*? Are you actually going to the library…on a Friday…in the summer…to look at micro*fiche*?"

Katey Jo was a good head taller than most kids in her class except Rosie. Turning fourteen in less than a month, she was the smartest kid in school… and dressed the part. She had straight black hair and never tried to do much with it. She wore glasses that made her look like a nerdy stereotype along with black-and-white Keds tennis shoes, bell-bottom jeans, and a rainbow-colored T-shirt. Full metal braces finished off the ensemble.

Thad cut his eyes at Katey Jo. "Yeah. Maybe."

"Thad, why would you guys wanna go to the library on a beautiful sunny day like this?" Allie asked sweetly.

Rosie leaned over to Marcus and whispered, "This is gonna be great."

Looking back at Allie, Thad opened his palm to reveal the pendant. Trying to sound mysterious, he said, "Uh…well, see, we found this necklace in the river by the old tire swing. We took it to Marcus's uncle Mike to see what it's worth. Turns out it may be tied to a missing girl named Abigail Lowery or something." Opening the locket, he showed Allie the inscription. "So I thought the library might be a good place to read about her."

"Abigail," she spoke while she read the words. "That sounds cool. Can we come?" Allie asked with a "no way to say no" smile.

"Sure…if you want," Thad responded with a "please please please" smile.

"Dude," Rosie said, directed at Thad as if to say "What are you thinking?"

Thad looked back at his two friends with a "help me" look.

Marcus jumped in. "Soooo…Katey Jo, you are in the library all the time. You know where all the microfiche is kept, don't you?" He guided her down the sidewalk towards the library.

Rosie fell in behind the two, walking past Allie and Thad, shaking his head.

Watching the others leave, Allie turned to Thad and made a funny face. "Take my picture."

"What? Oh…uh…my camera. Yeah, sure," Thad replied.

He held the Minolta to his eye and stared through the viewfinder. She was so beautiful. The sun shining off her hair. Her shirt making her eyes an even deeper blue than normal. She changed her funny face to a serious look and bit her lower lip ever so slightly. Thad clicked the shutter and captured a "real moment in time."

Allie laughed and gave him a quick kiss on the cheek and then turned and skipped to catch up to the others. Thad just stood there watching her, holding his cheek. He smiled like he knew a secret too good to tell and then took off toward the rest of his friends making their way to the library.

APPLE TARTS

"Two o'clock on the nose," Thad said to himself as he checked the time. The big EMPORIA PROUD sign still stood as it did years ago, the last time Thad was in town. He could see the Kiwanis, Civitans, and Lyons clubs needed to spruce up their placards a bit, but it still made him feel at home every time he passed them. There's a certain comfort in familiarity. Turning onto Sixth Avenue, he headed right into the heart of town. His mom's house was just off Sixth in a quaint, little two-bedroom shotgun home. It was the same home Thad grew up in. When he walked through the front door, it was like going back in time. Oval, jute mats decorated the hardwood floors like perfectly placed puddles of straw. There was the old picture of Jesus praying in the garden, the one with the halo around his head. It was hanging in the den in the same spot as long as Thad could remember. He bet if he lifted the frame, there would be an outline of it on the wallpaper. Clear plastic on the floral-printed sofa, a round oak dining room table with a bowl of fake fruit, and a built-in television cabinet completed the dated ensemble.

Thad tossed his bags on the sofa,. "Mom, I'm home!"

"William Thaddeus Taylor, is that you?" His mother called out from the kitchen.

"It's me," Thad answered.

Coming from the kitchen into the den, Mrs. Taylor said, "Oh my heaven's stars, let me look at you." Grabbing his face, she continued, "I swear you get better-looking every time I see you! You look just like your father…May he rest in peace."

After a long hug and a few kisses on his cheek, Thad held his mom at arm's length and said with a serious look on his face, "Mom, you know I love you, but this has to be said right now…I've got to pee."

With that, Thad let out a loud chuckle and his mom shooed him away with her kitchen towel.

"And you act just like your father…May he rest in peace."

"Ma, you don't have to say 'May he rest in peace' every time you mention Dad," Thad said on the way to the bathroom. "The man was a saint. If he ain't in peace, then no way in hell anyone else is."

"Thaddeus, I will not have blasphemy in this house," his mom warned. "If you talk like that, there will be no apple tarts for you!"

Walking into the kitchen while drying his hands on a towel he borrowed from the bathroom, Thad asked, "Apple tarts?"

"Yep," she replied.

"You mean the world-famous Mrs. Taylor's apple tarts?" he asked.

"Yes sirree," she answered.

Walking up to the oven and sniffing deeply in an attempt to almost consume the smell, Thad lengthened his question. "You mean the world-famous Mrs. Taylor's award-winning, best-tasting-in-the-universe apple tarts?"

"Yep," she replied with a cocky smile on her face.

"Well then, please forgive me, ma'am," Thad said with an apologetic grin.

The tart tasted like home. Sometimes his mom would make them on Sunday afternoons. After coming home from the Emporia First United Methodist Church, his mother would cook up a meal with enough food to feed half the neighborhood. Rosie was there at least every other Sunday, so on those days, there weren't as many leftovers. On those days, half the neighborhood would just have to wait until next Sunday.

"Lord knows growing boys can eat," she would always say.

The boys would hang around and watch football (always rooting for the Chiefs). Then they would play a game of tackle outside, just one-on-one, until Marcus started hanging around, then he was always the center/receiver, also known as the "hike it and go long" guy. Then Thad's mom would call them back inside for ice-cold whole milk and hot apple tarts. She would bring out the folding TV-trays, the kind with Wild West scenes painted on them, and turn the TV to *Mutual of Omaha's Wild Kingdom*. They would chow down on sweet apple tarts while they watched a crocodile chow down on a panicked, unfortunate zebra.

Those were the good ol' days to be sure. And with every bite, Thad could see Rosie sitting right there with him.

Man, I wish I could have had one more of my mom's apple tarts with you buddy, Thad thought.

But he knew what you'd get if you wished in one hand and spit in the other, so he just washed his last bite down with ice-cold whole milk and smiled at his mom while she explained why the ladies in her bridge club were one step above cutthroats and thieves. They sat at the old oak table and chatted about other things mothers and sons chat about. Three tarts later and nearly an hour of catch-up time, he excused himself for some well-deserved rest. He grabbed his bags and headed to his room. He also wanted to talk to Marcus and get some info on the funeral.

"Marcus, how's it going, brother?" Thad spoke into his cell phone.

"Doing all right, man," Marcus answered. "Just leaving the store. You made it yet?"

"Yep, just pulled in about an hour ago," Thad said, fighting back a yawn.

"Hey, you wanna go get a beer or something?" Marcus sounded his usual happy-go-lucky self.

"Maybe later. I've been on the road for hours. I'm beat," Thad said.

"Well, if you don't wanna get a beer, then I'm coming over tonight, amigo, and that's all there is to it," Marcus said. "Get yourself some rest. How about seven o'clock?"

Thad looked at his clock by his bed. *Gives me four hours' sleep*, he thought. "Make it eight," he told Marcus.

"Cool," Marcus said. "Think your mom could cook us up some apple tarts?"

Thad smiled but didn't let on that he had just devoured three of them. "I'm sure we can persuade her." Then he asked, "What are the particulars on the funeral tomorrow?"

"Funeral starts at three o'clock at the Palmer Brothers Funeral Home," Marcus said. "Us pallbearers need to be there at least thirty minutes early so I will meet you there a little before two thirty. Hey, you-know-who is gonna be there!"

"Shit, Marcus, don't go there," Thad warned. "I haven't seen her in years, and I'm sure she doesn't want me popping up at the inappropriate time with a cheesy 'how you been' line. Promise me you won't go play-ing matchmaker."

Marcus barely waited for Thad to finish. "But Allie's just got divorced from Danny McNeal, and I know for a fact she's not seeing anybody. She is still as pretty as ever, man—"

"Promise me, Marcus," Thad interrupted.

"But—" Marcus tried to start a sentence.

"Promise!" Thad said, more determined.

"Ok, I promise." Marcus sounded like a disappointed five-year-old.

After one more warning to Marcus about Allie, Thad told him he would see him later on that night and hung up the phone. He yelled out to his mother that Marcus was coming over for dinner, and then he crashed onto his bed and let out a long sigh. Staring up at the ceiling, he grabbed his old baseball still lying on his night table and tossed it up in the air.

"Allie Thompson...McNeal," he said to himself.

MICROFICHE

The Emporia Library was a classic old building, brick and mortar. A typical small-town library, it had all the classics but not so much any of the new stuff. You could find *The Catcher in the Rye* but good luck with Stephen King. It did, however, keep chronicles of old newspapers, and that's what they needed this day.

Thad held the door to let Allie go in ahead of him but the other kids took advantage of his gentlemanly manners.

"Thank you sir," Marcus said, "park the car around back." Acting as if he handed a set of keys to Thad.

This caused Rosie to laugh a little too loud bringing a stern glance from the librarian.

"Shush," Katey Jo said with her finger over her lips.

The boys quieted down and the kids walked past the front desk in single file. Katey Jo led the way and Thad brought up the rear. The librarian on duty was a breathing stereotype. She had silver hair in a bun, glasses on the tip of her nose held around her neck with a fancy chain, pencil in one hand, and a book in the other. She peered at the gaggle of kids as they made their way across the library. The stare she gave them left no doubt that she meant business. They instinctively went into tiptoe mode as they glided past the multitude of books. Katey Jo quietly led them down a flight of stairs to the lower level.

Standing in front of the filing cabinet, Katey Jo asked, "So you wanna see some microfiche? What exactly are you looking for?"

Thad answered, "We're not exactly sure. Some kind of newspaper story on a girl named Abigail Lowery. Like from 1956 maybe."

"Piece of cake," Katey Jo said confidently. "Let's just find the film for the *Emporia Gazette* from 1956."

"They have all that here?" Rosie asked.

Katey Jo looked at Rosie with a bewildered face. "Of course they do, silly."

"Yeah, silly," Marcus added, trying to sound learned.

"I'll pound your silly, stupid face in," Rosie threatened.

"Play nice, boys," Allie said in a motherly tone.

To Thad, she was intoxicating. He tried to act as normal as he could, but infatuation could hypnotize the mind and ensnare the heart. Staring at Allie like he was sleepwalking, Thad blurted out, "I'm a nice boy."

Instantly he knew he'd said something very embarrassing so he tried to cover it up. "Uh…I…mean…I'm playing with nice boys…uh…nice…I mean…Yeah, play nice boys." Apparently infatuation could fumble the tongue as well.

Rosie and Marcus both stared at their friend for a brief moment and then simultaneously busted out laughing.

"Shh, you're gonna get us thrown out of here," Katey Jo whispered. "Help me look for the *Gazette* from 1956 and…be quiet!"

After scrolling through the films for fifteen minutes or so, Thad stumbled upon an article.

"Hey! Check this out," Thad told the others.

"What'cha got?" Katey Jo asked.

"Something about a missing person...'Abigail Lowery was reported missing on May 20,'" Thad read aloud. "'Theparents woke up Sunday morning and their daughter was gone'."

"That's it!" Rosie said with excitement. "What else does it say?"

Thad continued, "It says 'The police are treating the case as a possible runaway, but the parents insist their daughter would never run away.' That's about all."

"It's dated May 21," Allie said. "Let's check for some more dates a few days out."

The kids combed through a few more rolls and found several more stories regarding Abigail Lowery. One told how her friend Ellen went to the police to tell how she was supposed to get a call from Abigail to come pick her up at a gas station. They were going to go to a campout, but Abigail never called so Ellen figured she chickened out. She waited a few days to come to the police because she was afraid she would get into trouble. Another one told how an all-out search took place. Police, FBI, friends, and neighbors, even hound dogs, were all searching for her for weeks. But in the end...nothing, not one trace of Abigail Lowery, an unsolved mystery.

Rosie looked up from the last article. "Hmm, 1956. That's like..."

It was easy to tell he was doing the math in his head.

"Nineteen years ago?" Katey Jo said.

"I knew that," Rosie answered almost immediately.

Thad said, "Let's look up stuff on the Cottonwood Killer, too."

"The Cottonwood Killer?" Katey Jo asked

"Uncle Mike said the cops thought he might be involved but could never tie him to Abigail," Marcus said. "He kidnapped and killed like nine other girls and tossed them in the Cottonwood."

"Sicko," Allie said.

They looked for information on the Cottonwood Killer and eventually found some articles from the 1960s that told how he was caught. He was an eccentric artist who painted portraits and river scenes. He lived about five miles west of Emporia on an old farm. His last kidnapping victim escaped and helped the police find him. He had been found guilty in the kidnapping of ten girls and the murder of nine. The police suspected him in the disappearance of Abigail, but he never confessed and they never found her body. He was hung in 1964. His name was Leonard Gauford.

Thad had an idea. Looking at Rosie and Marcus, he said, "Guys, why don't we go looking for her? We could tell our folks we're camping out in the tree house for the weekend. We can go back to the tire swing and look around." Both of his friends looked excited about the adventure.

Marcus spoke up. "Maybe we could find her bones. That would be so cool!"

"I've never seen a real live skeleton before," Rosie said.

"Technically," Katey Jo said with a teacher's tone, "it's a real dead skeleton."

Rosie gave her a sarcastic smile.

"Guys, come on," Thad said with a solemn voice. "Let's show some respect. Plus, we'll probably never find her anyway."

"You don't know that," Marcus said.

Allie said, "We wanna come. Katey Jo, you could tell your parents you're staying at my place, and I could tell mine I'm staying at yours!"

"Really? You want to come with us?" Thad asked sheepishly.

"Why not?" Katey Jo smirked. "Think we're too scared or something?"

"No, I don't think that," Thad responded.

"Good. Then it's settled," Allie said. "Meet up in Peter Pan Park, say… seven o'clock? See you boys then."

The girls turned to leave the library.

Rosie raised his voice to the girls. "Bring some snacks and a sleeping bag…and a flashlight!"

As the girls bounced away, the boys planned out their weekend. They would start at the river, head over to the old tire swing, camp, and see what else they could scrounge up.

But first the boys decided to head to the police department to see what they could find out from the chief of police, Sam Smith, or "Smitty," as the whole town knew him. Chief Smitty had been on the force since the sixties. He was there when they arrested Leonard Gauford. If any-one knew anything about Abigail Lowery, it would be the chief.

Leaving the library, Thad couldn't help but think of Allie Thompson and how soft her lips felt on his cheek. *This is definitely going to be an adventure*, he thought.

GREEN GRASS AND SCREEN DOOR LOCKS

Marcus pulled up to Mrs. Taylor's house just after sunset. He parked his truck right in the front yard, just like when they were teenagers. Back then, it was not uncommon to drive by Thad's house and find four or more cars parked in the yard: Rosie's, Marcus's, Allie's, and of course Thad's. Mr. Taylor used to say his lawn looked like a used car lot.

Marcus left the key in the ignition and walked to the front door. He noticed the front porch could use a paint job. It wasn't awful, but it could use a little sprucing up. He was surprised he hadn't noticed it before. Mrs. Taylor was like a mother to him. After Mr. Taylor died, Marcus felt a duty to keep an eye on her. He knew Thad was working all over the world and could not be there for his mom as much as he wanted, so Marcus would stop by after work at least once a week. She would have supper waiting for him. She would talk his ear off about this and that. There would usually be a comment about the cheats in her bridge club. She would always tell Marcus he needed to come to church with her on Sunday, he usually agreed but rarely complied. He never said much. He just listened, except he would always tell her a new joke before he left, and she would always laugh and tell him he was the funniest person she knew. Yes, he loved her like a mother. She filled a void in his life that he longed for, growing up without a mother, and he gave her the ability to nurture someone. A very symbiotic relationship if there ever was one.

He scratched a small chip of paint off of the case moulding around the door. "Definitely gonna get on this," he said to himself, taking note of the color. He opened the screen door and knocked on the oak one. He did not wait for a reply. He opened the heavy door wide enough to stick his head in.

"Mrs. Taylor, it's me," Marcus said loud enough for anyone in the home to hear. He took a step inside the house.

"Hey, sweetie," Mrs. Taylor said as she walked out of the kitchen, meeting him in the living room.

He gave her a kiss on the cheek and promptly stuck his nose up in the air.

He sniffed and said, "Mmm, something smells deee-licious."

"I hope you're hungry, Marcus. I cooked up enough food to last the week," Mrs. Taylor said.

"Yes, ma'am, I am," Marcus replied. "Where's that no-good son of yours?"

Mrs. Taylor smiled. "He's in his room," she answered. "Been sleeping for several hours. I was about to go wake him up for dinner."

"No, no, let me do it," Marcus said with a grin.

"Ok," she said, "tell him we eat in fifteen minutes."

Marcus agreed and tiptoed down the hall to Thad's room. He opened the door and entered the room with the deftness of a psycho killer straight out of a horror movie. Seeing Thad sleeping so innocently, he smiled an evil-genius smile. Looking around the room, he sized up his possible weapons of choice. There was a baseball bat standing in the corner, probably too heavy to use without damaging something. On the dresser he saw a tambourine from the days when Thad wanted to join a band. He chuckled quietly to himself at the thought. A metal trashcan, an alarm clock, and a lamp were available if need be. But then he saw it hanging on the lamp-shade. The perfect weapon—a whistle. He knew it was from Thad's years as a lifeguard. He gently lifted the whistle so as not to awaken his victim. As quiet as a mouse, he inched closer and closer to the sleeping beauty, who snored with every breath. Marcus raised the whistle to his mouth and pressed it between his lips. Bending over to within a foot of Thad's ear, he took a deep breath. With one forceful exhale, all hell broke loose.

At the blistering sound, Thad sat straight up and screamed like a twelve-year-old girl. His forehead bumped hard into Marcus's head, sending Marcus flying backward toward the dresser. Marcus's backside hit the dresser with enough force to cause the lamp to go sailing toward its ultimate doom. It crashed upon the floor, becoming an instant jigsaw puzzle. While all of this happened, Thad grabbed his forehead and jumped out of bed. He stepped on the baseball lying on the floor. Losing his balance he flew face-first into Marcus's crotch. Both men hit the floor, Thad still holding his forehead and Marcus holding his forehead…and his groin.

"Owww," Marcus said.

"What the hell?" Thad screamed.

"What's going on in there?" The men heard Mrs. Taylor yell down the hall. "Everybody ok?"

"We are fine, Mom," Thad yelled back.

"Hey, buddy," Marcus said to Thad with an "oops" expression.

Thad wanted to punch him in the face, but he started laughing at what the previous few seconds must have looked like. Marcus joined in and before long the two friends were laughing hard and holding their wounded body parts.

"Mom's gonna beat your ass when she sees what you did to the lamp," Thad said, still laughing.

"Aww, we can use a little super glue and buff this right out." Marcus laughed, trying to fit two of the dozen or so fallen pieces together.

"How the hell you been Marcus?" Thad asked as the laughter wound down.

"Been good pods," he answered. "How 'bout you?"

"I'm good, except I miss this place…miss hanging out with you guys," Thad answered. He instantly thought of not being able to hang out with Rosie anymore.

"Me, too," Marcus said. He paused for a second and continued, "Your mom said dinner is ready and to get your lazy ass out of bed."

"Lazy ass?" Thad said. "My mom doesn't say 'ass.'"

"I'm paraphrasing," Marcus said, "and that doesn't mean she doesn't think you're one."

"Ha ha," Thad said. "Better get to the table if we wanna eat."

"Last one there has to wash dishes," Marcus said, springing up and dashing out of the room.

Thad was right behind him as the two hustled to be the first one to the dinner table.

"You two act like kids," Mrs. Taylor said, setting the pot roast on the table.

She set the rest of the dishes on the oak table to join the roast. There were new potatoes and carrots in beef gravy. Corn on the cob, complete with holders and little corn-shaped trays to soak them in salt and butter. Macaroni and cheese and field peas, too. You could sop up the gravy with buttered dinner rolls. And of course, she had apple tarts for dessert.

"Mom, how many folks did you think were coming?" Thad asked as he dug into the fixings.

"Well, I don't get to cook as much as I used to," she answered. "If sweet Marcus didn't come by like he does, I probably wouldn't cook anything. And I love to cook for my boys."

She pinched Marcus's cheek. He blushed a little and grabbed an ear of corn. He went to take a bite when he heard Mrs. Taylor tell him to wait.

"Marcus Pawley," she said like only a mother could, "you know we say grace in this house before we eat God's bounty."

"Yes, ma'am," he said, putting the corn back into its tray.

"Thad, will you do the honors?" she asked her son.

They all bowed their heads and folded their hands. Thad wanted to get this over with quick and tear into the meal his mother had cooked, but he thought of Rosie and decided to really pray for a change.

"Dear Heavenly Father," Thad began, "thank you for this meal and for the one who prepared it. Please continue to watch over her and keep her safe. Thank you for family and friends, and God, please take care of them. Please take care of Rosie. There've been many times he sat right here at this table with us and shared a meal. It's going to be tough without him. Help Linda and the kids through this difficult time. I can only imagine how hard this must be for them."

Thad paused for a moment as he felt a tear ever so slightly begin to form in the corner of his eye. He decided to wrap up the prayer or he would lose it right then and there. "Please bless this food to our bodies and our bodies to your service. In Christ's name I pray. Amen."

Everyone followed with an "Amen" and the feast began.

Dinner plates and catching up go hand in hand. Marcus told Thad about everything that happened with Allie, pitching the dirt about her break-up and what a douchebag her ex-husband was. Marcus told him KJ was coming in from Alaska. He told him about the Cottonwood being at record lows, and how the meat factory was placing a plaque near the entrance for Rosie. He told him about the crazy things that had come through his pawnshop over the last year, including a set of gold teeth to pay for a divorce.

"I had a guy try to pawn his kidney stone," Marcus said with a mouthful of pot roast. "A kidney stone!"

Marcus told stories about the Three Amigos and how they would all end up in a barn or a pool hall or the girls' locker room. Mrs. Taylor would hide her eyes in shame and slap Thad with a napkin at the tales. Everyone at the table was laughing, which was fine with Thad. It's hard to distinguish a sad tear from a happy one.

Thad just sat, laughed, and listened. He loved his hometown. He loved his friends. He already missed Rosie.

"Once you've got small town in your blood, you never get it out of ya," his dad used to tell him. "They all come back eventually," he would say, "whether it's to live or to die, they all come back."

It was a good night. It was good to see Marcus being Marcus, all goofy and talkative. It was good to sit down with his mom and eat the best meal he had had in what seemed like forever. They all walked outside after dinner, and Thad stood on the front lawn. It was a warm night. He was barefoot. He couldn't even remember the last time he went barefoot in DC. The grass felt cool beneath his toes as the dew worked its way up the green blades.

Marcus kissed Mrs. Taylor on the cheek and slapped Thad on the back before he got into his truck.

"See ya tomorrow at two thirty," he said to Thad.

He climbed into driver's seat, turned the ignition, and leaned out the window.

"Hey, Mrs. T," he said turning down his radio. "What do you call a guy who never farts in public?" He gave her a second and then answered. "A private tutor. Get it? A tutor."

"You are so funny," Mrs. Taylor said laughing.

Marcus laughed at his own jokes like he heard them for the first time. Mrs. Taylor laughed, too, and Marcus loved that. Thad rolled his eyes and chuckled. He wasn't always big on Marcus's jokes, but he was big on how much he looked after his mom, so in Thad's book, Marcus was his brother. His last living brother, and they were burying his only other brother tomorrow.

"You coming inside?" Mrs. Taylor asked Thad as Marcus drove off.

"In a minute, Mom," he said.

She kissed him on the cheek and left him in the front yard. He squished the grass between his toes and smiled at how much stress it seemed to take away.

With his hands in his pockets and his eyes turned to the sky, he spoke. "Missed you tonight, Rosie," he said.

He didn't have to say anything else. That summed it all up. He missed his lost brother, period. He turned back to the house and closed the screen door behind him. He was placing the screen door latch in the hook but then stopped, looked outside, and let it hang loose. One of the perks of living in a small town. He closed the door and turned off the lights. Nothing like being home, really being home.

CHATTING WITH THE CHIEF

Rosie took the lead as the boys left the library and meandered their way through downtown Emporia. Heading to the police station, Thad wore a big smile, thinking about the kiss on the cheek he received earlier. He wondered if Allie really would show up tonight. *How awesome would that be?* he thought.

He imagined Allie and himself sitting around a campfire by the old tire swing. Maybe he would get a chance to hold her hand. Maybe even a chance for a kiss…a real kiss, not one on the cheek. Then reality hit him. He'd never kissed a girl. He had no idea how to even go about it. To Thad, girls were like the cosmos, beautiful to look at it but difficult to navigate. What would he do if she gave him signals, and what exactly were the signals? The thought almost panicked him.

"What are you doing?" Rosie asked Thad. "You're face looks retarded."

Thad realized he was caught somewhere between a smile and a look of fear.

"What are you talking about?" he asked, trying to deflect the obvious.

"He's got gas," Marcus said, laughing.

"Whatever," Thad fired back. "Look who's talking Mr. Fart-alot-us."

Rosie grabbed Thad by the shoulders, squinted his eyes, concentrated hard and let one rip. At the sound of methane escaping from his body, the boys lost it and had to stop walking until the laughs ran their course. Like all boys, nothing made the three amigos laugh harder than fart humor. Thad was glad the conversation took a turn in a new direction. He didn't feel like getting the ribbing he was sure to receive from his buddies if they knew the truth. After the laughter and odor subsided, they continued their trek to the station.

The three friends walked into the Emporia Police Department as if they had been there a time or two. Actually, they had never been in trouble with the law. They knew the building from a school field trip they took back in the early spring. They even knew where Chief Smitty's office was. Shuffling their way past the front desk, they turned down the hall to the chief.

"Hold it, you three," a booming voice said from behind them.

The boys stopped in their tracks and turned to see all six foot five inches, two hundred and fifty pounds of Sergeant Kyle standing behind them with his arms folded and his eyebrows raised.

"Where do you think you're going?" Sergeant Kyle asked.

"Umm, we want to see Chief Smitty," Marcus said.

"The chief is busy," the sergeant said. "Why do you want to see him anyway?"

Thad answered. "We want to ask him about an old case, a case from the fifties and sixties."

"You're Bill Taylor's boy, aren't you?" the sergeant asked, looking down at Thad.

"Yes, sir. I'm Thad."

"He joined the Masonic Lodge the same time I did," Sergeant Kyle said, taking a more pleasant tone. "What would make three teenage boys want to play detective on a beautiful summer afternoon?"

Not wanting to give their hand away, Thad came up with a somewhat truthful answer. "We were just hanging out in the library looking through old microfiche and found a story about a girl named Abigail Lowery who went missing in the fifties. We wanted to know if the chief remembered anything about her."

"The library?" the sergeant asked, not exactly believing Thad's story.

"Yes, sir," Thad answered. "We are starting high school this year and want to get a jump-start on our civics class. Try to impress the teacher, you know?"

The sergeant figured the boys were up to something, but he was too busy to snoop any further.

"Guys, I think it's cool that you are interested in studying old case files," Sergeant Kyle said, "but the chief is just too busy. Best to keep your research confined to the library."

"I'm too busy for what?" Chief Smitty asked, walking up behind the sergeant.

"Hi, Chief," the sergeant said with surprise. "These boys were wantin' to talk to you about an old case, but I explained to them that you were too busy."

Chief Smitty was known to be one of the friendliest persons in the town of Emporia. Everybody liked him. He was affable, charismatic, and honest. Thad remembered how nice he was to their class on the field trip. He took extra time to answer everybody's questions, locked

Rosie up in the jail for a few minutes, and even let every student take a turn at sounding the siren in a real squad car.

"Hey, fellas," the chief said to the boys.

"Hi," the boys said in unison.

"Weren't you guys here a few months ago on the field trip?" Chief Smitty asked.

"Yes, sir," Rosie said. "You locked me in the jail cell. It was awesome!"

The chief laughed. "I remember. You're name is…" the chief said, tapping his index finger to his lips, "Rosie. Right?"

"That's right," Rosie said, surprised. That was another one of the chief's attributes. He had the ability to put names and faces together like magic. It came from years of working his way up from beat cop to detective to captain and eventually chief of police. Plus, Rosie was easy to remember; he was a big kid with an unusual name. A piece of cake for the likes of Chief Smitty.

"And you're Marcus, aren't you?" the chief said, pointing to Marcus. He would have liked to say it was because of his recognition powers, but honestly it was because he had been to Marcus's house more that once on a domestic disturbance call over the years. He knew young Marcus had it tough, and he had a soft spot in his heart for kids that had it tough.

"I'm Thad," Thad said, not wanting to be left out.

The chief laughed. "That's right, you are." He turned to Sergeant Kyle. "I might have a couple of minutes to spare, Sergeant. Why don't you take these fellas to the interrogation room and get them some Cokes."

The three boys looked at one another, smiling, eyes wide with excitement at the words "interrogation room" and "Cokes."

"Yes, sir, Chief," the sergeant replied in a distinctly military tone.

The interrogation room was as nondescript as it could be. It was lit with florescent bulbs tucked into latticework casings. The concrete block walls were painted pale green. There was a long table in the middle of the room with six chairs placed randomly around it. One wall had a large mirror cut into it, but the boys knew it was a two-way mirror, which allowed the detectives to watch from another room. The sergeant escorted the three kids into the room and headed to the vending machine to get the sodas as ordered. Marcus walked up to the mirror and stuck his tongue out and his finger up his nose.

"Cut it out, stupid," Rosie said. "What if somebody's on the other side?"

"Then they're probably laughing," Marcus said. He turned his head sideways and pressed it against the mirror leaving an imprint of his profile.

"That's a good position for you," Thad said. "They make prisoners turn their head to take their pictures."

Rosie and Thad laughed as the door opened and Chief Smitty entered the room. They straightened up quickly and turned to the chief.

"Take a seat, boys," the chief said.

The three kids sat down on one side of the table, the chief sat on the other.

"Now what about this old case?" the chief asked.

Thad took the lead. "Well, sir," he said, "see, we were at the library looking at microfiche, and we read about this missing girl from the fifties named Abigail Lowery. We were wondering if you knew anything about that case."

The chief furled his eyebrows. "Abigail Lowery," he said, letting his mind drift back. "I remember her. She went missing a few years after I joined the force. We never found her."

"The newspaper said that you guys thought that a man named Leonard Gaylord might have been the one to take her," Thad said, "but no one could ever prove it."

"Leonard Gauford." The chief corrected Thad. He was a genius with names. "We were sure he was in on her disappearance, but the guy never confessed. We got him on the kidnapping and murder of nine other girls plus another kidnapping. I was there when we arrested him. I never will forget it." The chief looked at all three boys and asked, "Why are you boys reading microfiche about Abigail Lowery?"

"Just interested in detective stuff," Thad said, "and gettin' ready for our civics class."

"Yeah, we start high school this year," Rosie said.

"Hmm," the chief said.

The door opened and Sergeant Kyle entered the room with three Coca-Colas. He set them on the table in front of the boys and excused himself. The kids pulled off the tabs and placed the pop-tops on the table. All three took a sip.

Marcus followed his up with, "Ahhhh."

The break in conversation allowed Thad to get the chief back on the subject. "What do you think happened to her?"

"Well," Chief Smitty answered, "the guy was known as the Cottonwood Killer because he placed the girls in and around the river. She fit the profile for the type of girl he went after...teenager...pretty...alone at night. Odds are he took her. If so, she would have probably been dumped somewhere near or in the river. We looked up and down the Cottonwood, but there was never anything found, not even way down-stream. She just disappeared. Her parents went to their graves never knowing what happened to her. It was sad boys, real sad."

"Has it been too long to find her now?" Marcus asked.

"Well, after all this time, there wouldn't be much to find. A skeleton would be all that's left and probably not all together, unless she was buried," the chief answered. "That was not his M.O. though. He usually dumped the bodies. But the FBI said that if Abigail was his first victim, he might have buried her."

"What's an M.O.?" Rosie asked.

The chief smiled. "Modus operandi," he explained. "The way someone usually does things."

"Ohhhh," Rosie said.

"So she may be buried near the Cottonwood River?" Thad asked.

"It is possible," the chief answered.

The three boys looked at one another.

"Well, boys I really need to get back to it. Keep up the detective work and let me know if you find anything," Chief Smitty said with a chuckle.

He escorted the teenagers out of the room and to the front door. He said goodbye to the kids as they headed out of the building.

"He said she might be buried near the Cottonwood," Rosie said with excitement as they walked to the sidewalk.

"I bet she is buried near the tire swing," Marcus said. "This is gonna be so spooky-cool tonight. I bet we find her."

"Maybe," Thad said, "but it has been twenty years and who knows where she really is?"

"But we do have her necklace, so that means she should be near where we found it," Rosie argued.

"True," Thad said, playing the devil's advocate, "if that really is her necklace."

"It is," Marcus's said. "It is."

They stopped at the corner and went over the particulars of the evening one more time. It was hot, but the temperature was supposed to cool down a good bit in the evening, so they made sure to wear long sleeves. The sun was making its way well past the halfway mark in the sky, casting longer and longer shadows on everything it touched. Marcus headed to his house and Thad and Rosie turned toward their street. Devil's advocate or not, Thad was excited about the prospect of looking for Abigail Lowery…and the prospect of kissing Allie Thompson.

STINGS LIKE HELL

The crowd at the Emporia First United Methodist Church was a decent size. "Probably better than I'll get," Thad said to himself. He and Marcus did their duty as pallbearers along with a couple of Rosie's in-laws and two nephews. Thad noticed Allie sitting in the pew when he entered with the other pallbearers, but the time wasn't right to give her a smile, so he kept his head forward and moved into the assigned pew.

"And the Bible says 'Oh death, where is your victory? Where is your sting?'" The pastor rolled the words off his tongue.

Pastor, it stings like hell, Thad thought.

Looking over his shoulder, he saw Marcus tilting his sunglasses back and forth with his finger placed behind his ear causing the funny motion to occur. He gave Thad that completely inappropriate Hollywood grin. *Marcus hasn't changed a bit,* Thaddeus thought. Thad looked at him as if to say, "Take those off. You're indoors, you idiot." Marcus slowed the motion down to a stop, put the glasses in his coat pocket, and turned back to the preacher. Thad did smile, but he would not let Marcus see it. Ever since they were kids, the third part of the trio was the funny man. Thad was the intellectual-artist type, Rosie was the tough guy, and Marcus...well, let's just say Marcus had a way of always getting them in trouble while laughing their guts out about it at the same time.

Thad remembered one time when they were hanging out at the baseball field one summer. Little League was in full force. None of them played, all though every coach tried to recruit Rosie. They did like to come watch an occasional game from time to time, munch on a hot dog, down a bottle of Coke, and yell insults at whichever team name they disliked the most. Of course they would check out any girls in the stands. Except for one incredibly talented golden retriever used as a batboy, the game on this day was a real stink-o, and they were getting bored. Marcus suddenly came up with a brilliant idea.

"Guys, I got it," Marcus said. "Oh, I got it. This one will be awesome. I'm talking front-page-news awesome."

"Marcus, what are you talking about?" Rosie asked.

"Yeah? Front-page news?" Thad added.

Marcus, barely able to contain his excitement, said, "Streaking! Let's streak across the field!"

"Streaking?" Rosie said. "You are out of your mind."

"Yeah, you've had one too many Coca-Colas," Thad said.

"Come on, guys," Marcus said. "It will be legendary. Imagine everyone's faces when three white butts go running across the pitcher's mound."

"No way, man," Thad said.

"Wait a minute, Thad, he might be on to something," Rosie said, winking at Thad out of Marcus's sight.

"Yeah, I'm on to something!" Marcus stood up smiling, even more excited.

Realizing Rosie had a trick up his sleeve, Thad joined in. "Yeah, you're right. That would be freaking awesome. Let's do it!"

Amazed at his ability to convince his friends, Marcus said, "Cool, let's go behind the visitors' dugout where nobody is. We can lose our clothes there, take off across the field, and loop back around. We can grab our clothes when we get back to the dugout and haul butt outta here!"

The other two quickly agreed, and they took off toward the dugout.

Lagging behind Marcus, Thad whispered to Rosie, "What are we doing, man?"

"When he takes off running, we take off the other way!" Rosie said under his breath.

Thad gave a big grin and a nod, and they continued to the dugout. Once there, they scouted the area for busybodies, but none were to be found. The three boys quickly disrobed down to their underwear and placed their clothes in a pile.

Marcus looked around and then at his friends. "Ok, on the count of three, let's drop the skivvies and run like a bat out of hell." He could barely control himself at this point. The other two shook their heads in agreement.

"One...two...*three!*"

All three boys dropped their briefs. Marcus took off first, heading for the pitcher's mound and yelling like his hair was on fire. The other two pulled up their drawers, grabbed all the clothes, and took off for the woods. By the time Marcus realized he was on his own, it was too late. One grandmother screamed. A dad covered his daughter's eyes. Over the microphone, the announcer yelled, "Protect the women and children!" The catcher completely missed the pitch, and the runner on second took off toward third. Marcus had no choice but to turn to the outfield; however, he didn't take into account the height of the fence. An eight-foot-tall chain-link fence and a five-foot-tall, naked fourteen-year-old do not mix. He bounced off the fence and veered toward home plate with two coaches, six ball players, and one golden retriever hot on his tail.

Thad and Rosie watched it all from the woods, fully clothed and laughing hysterically. Eventually Marcus bolted out of the ball field and headed to the dugout. He was stunned to find no clothes waiting for him. He veered toward the woods, looking for the closest cover he could find. He heard Thad and Rosie calling his name, so he tore out in their direction. They all three dashed through the woods until they could hear no more commotion. They stopped running to catch their breath.

"You guys are assholes!" Marcus said, jerking his clothes from Rosie's hands.

"Maybe so," Thad said with his hands on his knees, breathing heavily, "but at least no one saw ours!"

Thad and Rosie hit the ground laughing, and eventually Marcus started chuckling, letting it roll into full-fledged laughter…

Thad caught himself laughing out loud a little during the service. Marcus looked over at him with an expression of "What?" on his face. Embarrassed, Thad glanced around to make sure no one had noticed as he surreptitiously slipped back into the preacher's sermon.

All in all it was a beautiful service. After they drove from the church to the cemetery and laid Rosie's body to rest, Thad gave his condolences to Linda and the kids at the graveside.

"He loved you like a brother," Linda told him.

"He was my brother," Thad replied.

He kissed her on the cheek and turned away. He stopped and placed his hand on Rosie's casket, clearing his throat several times. He found this was the best way to hold back tears.

"I will see you again one day, my friend," he said in a whisper.

Walking his mother back to the car, Thad saw Allie again but conveniently found a way to "accidentally" miss her. It was like her fourteenth birthday party all over again.

"Isn't that Allie Thompson over there?" his mother asked a little too rhetorically.

"Yes, Mother, it is," Thad said, steering her toward the car.

"She still looks lovely, don't you think, Thaddeus?" his mother said, obviously trying to start something, looking back over her shoulder while Thad moved her along.

"She's gorgeous," Thad said quickly. "Now can we get going?"

Just then Marcus caught up with them. "Hi, Mrs. Taylor," he said. "Thad, check out Allie Thompson."

"I see her already," Thad said, obviously frustrated, "would everybody get out of my hair?"

Thad left his mother to Marcus's care and headed to the car, taking large, fast steps.

"What'd I say?" Marcus asked, looking at Mrs. Taylor.

There was not one mention of "Allie Thompson" in the car as Thad, his mother, and Marcus drove back to Rosie's house where there would be an abundance of food. Somehow gnawing on a fried chicken leg and swallowing spoonfuls of banana pudding seemed to make the parade of death easier to stomach.

Thad was working on his second drumstick when he felt a tap on his right shoulder. Turning around with half a chicken leg attached to his lips, he saw Allie standing right in front of him with as beautiful a smile as ever.

"So," she said, "you planning on ignoring me all day?"

Embarrassed but covert, he answered, "Allie Thompson…McNeal! Wow! You look great. Ignoring you? Nooo. I was just wrapped up in the pall-bearer stuff, you know." He followed his lame excuse with a guilty grin.

"Of course," Allie replied with one eyebrow raised. "I know you wouldn't avoid me. The funeral was beautiful wasn't it? And it's just Allie Thompson now."

"Oh, that's right," Thad said, "I heard about you and Danny. Sorry, Allie."

"I'm not," she said, brushing the topic away like a piece of lint. "Listen, Katey Jo's in town and I'm meeting up with her at Phil's Grill tonight. You should come hang out and bring Marcus. It'll be like old times…almost."

Thad could tell she was thinking of Rosie.

"How about 8:00?" She asked.

"Uh, sure, sounds wonderful," Thad answered.

Marcus appeared suddenly. "What sounds wonderful?"

Allie smiled. "You, Thad, Katey Jo, and me at Phil's tonight at eight o'clock."

She gave both boys a kiss on their cheeks and headed to say goodbye to Linda.

Thad looked at Marcus with a stare of blame.

"Hey, I didn't do anything here," Marcus said defensively. "Fate has a way of tossing it high and inside, buddy!"

"Yes it does, amigo, yes it does," Thad said as he watched Allie exit the room.

AS TOUGH AS SHE WAS BEAUTIFUL

She caught herself daydreaming, staring into her dressing mirror. She had been thinking about Rosie, Marcus, Katey Jo and Thad, especially Thad. She snapped back to attention. Allie Thompson was as tough as she was beautiful. The daughter of a military man, she was used to moving around and following orders. Texas, California, Georgia, North Dakota, even a stint in Guam…these were just a few stops along the road of her young life. Living in so many different places taught her a few things. One was to be guarded, two was to be friendly, and three was to kick anybody's ass when necessary.

One time in the third grade, a navy lieutenant's son kept picking on her. She warned him repeatedly, but honestly talking to an eight-year-old boy is like talking to an eight-year-old monkey; the only difference is a monkey listens better.

When he finally said, "Marines are losers," she snapped. It took two teachers to pull her off of him. He was losing blood from his nose and tears from his eyes.

"Looks like sailors are the losers today," she said as they dragged her away, still kicking and screaming, to the principal's office. Her dad scolded her in front of the principal, but when he got her in the car, he started grinning like only a proud father can.

"Let's go get us an ice cream," he said, beaming.

She smiled at her dad and sarcastically said, "Sailors."

Her father finally settled his family down in the town of Emporia, Kansas, when she was ten years old. He ran the local marine recruitment office. Her grandfather was a marine. Her dad was a marine. Her older brother was currently a marine, but the lifestyle wasn't for her. That didn't mean she didn't have immense respect for the profession; it was just that she wanted children…and a husband…and a fixed location for a home. *Two outta three ain't bad,* she always thought, but now, after the divorce, she was down to a third.

She was a real estate agent, and a damn good one at that. That's how she found her home on the Cottonwood River. It was an old farmhouse fixer-upper, but she loved the bones of the place and was committed to making it her dream home. She could sell a house with the best of them. Her name was always on top of the "sales of the month" board hanging in the break room. She was agent of the year three years running. The women in the office blamed it on her looks, the men blamed it on her brown-nosing, but Allie knew it was a mixture of psychology and skill. She figured four years in college and a BS in Psychology was good for something. It may not have been as grandiose as say, teaching Psych 101 at Harvard, but at least she was able to have a good home, a nice car, and nice clothes.

She had been pregnant with a son. "My future general," her dad would say. Her father never served much praise on her husband, Danny; in fact, he thought he was a sorry sack of shit, but when he found out that his only daughter was pregnant—and with a boy, no less—he slapped Danny on the back and said, "Way to go, son. I didn't think you had it in you." Allie really thought the baby would fix what was wrong between Danny and her. She imagined a doting father and a laughing boy playing baseball in the yard. No more drinking. No more fights. No more getting fired from his job. No more running around. But that was a hell of a tall order for a baby boy, even if he was a marine. Throughout the pregnancy, the fights continued. Danny spent more time on their couch than he did drawing a paycheck. Allie would often come home from work to find him sleeping on the sofa, empty beer cans on the floor and the TV tuned into country music videos.

They say the chance of losing a child after the twentieth week of pregnancy is less than 1 percent. The bleeding started when she was five months along. She lost her son two weeks later. No one is to blame for a stillbirth, but no one bears the burden like a mother. She cried. She got angry at God. She even wrote her unborn son a letter, asking for his forgiveness for not being strong enough to bring him life. Time is a good healer, but some wounds slice deeper than others. Still, Allie Thompson was as tough as she was beautiful, and she soldiered on.

Two years and countless fights later, she and Danny finally called it what it was: over. The divorce was a messy one. It ended up with a jury hearing all the details of their dirty laundry. Alley was mortified. She was always so well put together, and having her life disintegrate in front of the whole town was horrible. But she was as tough as she was beautiful, so she fought for what she thought was right. They both wanted the house and Danny wanted alimony since she made more money than him. However, his years of sloth and philandering did not sit well with the jury. She got the house and the car. He got no alimony and a vengeful attitude. Thirty-one days later the gavel came down, and they were no longer husband and wife. "Let no man put asunder," unless he is a judge of the great state of Kansas.

She opened the doors to her closet and blew her breath up toward her bangs in frustration. Picking up this outfit and that one, never satisfied with what she saw. Holding one in front of a mirror and then another. She and her wardrobe kept up the dance for twenty minutes.

"Jesus, Allie, you're not going to the prom. Just pick one," she said to no one.

Finally, she settled on something that said she was sophisticated but just daring enough to be interesting.

Her makeup table was a disaster. Concealer intertwined with perfume. Lipstick hiding underneath a curling iron. A powder puff fighting with a foundation brush. Max Factor would be highly disappointed. It was ironic really, considering how neat she was in every other single aspect of her life. She rationalized it was the "one thing" she could let go. Kind of an escape valve. But the reality is that she hated the business of cosmetically enhancing one's self. That did not mean she wouldn't use it; it just made her a hypocrite in her own eyes. The crazy thing is, Allie Thompson was absolutely beautiful with no makeup on. Five foot five, 130 pounds, slim but curvy build, a youthful face, wide and bright blue eyes that complemented her high cheekbones, long blond hair… everything that made her a picture-perfect girl next door.

"You're slipping, girl," she told herself as she stared at the crow's feet crawling their way around the corners of her eyes. She pulled her eyes back to make the lines disappear and would watch them reappear as soon as she let go.

Why did she tell Thad that she and Katey Jo were going out tonight? *What was I thinking?*

She just got out of one relationship, and the last thing she needed right now was another one with a man who lived a thousand miles away.

Lining her eyes meticulously, she said out loud, "Relationship? It's just drinks with an old friend," as she stared at her face in the mirror, trying to convince herself of just that.

But this was not just an "old friend." This was Thad Taylor. Her first love. The man she thought she was going to run away with after school to start a perfect life together. She still remembered his soft kisses and his strong hands on her body. She would close her eyes when Danny would make love to her and imagine he was Thad. It used to make her feel guilty, but over time it just made her feel nothing, at least for her ex-husband.

"He lives in DC, you live in Emporia," she said to herself as she ran the large, round brush through her long, silky hair. "It's been years. Get over it. It ain't gonna happen."

Slipping the white V-neck blouse over her head, she gave herself one last check in the mirror. She adjusted both breasts to "even" them up. "Maybe not twenty-two, but they are still perky," she thought. She turned to look at her butt in her denims. Still firm, but then again the jeans were so tight they would hold anything in place, at least that's what she told herself. She put her face close to mirror and pulled on her crow's feet one more time. "Damn," she said.

She punched Katey Jo's number into her phone and told her she was on her way. "Let's go have one for Rosie, and two for us," she told Katey Jo, sounding like an old Irish toastmaster. With that, she hung up the phone, grabbed her keys, and marched out the door, tough and beautiful.

SOME FIGHTS AREN'T FAIR

Thinking about the possibility of finding someone's bones must make a person pick up their pace. It seemed to Marcus that he had just left his two friends outside the police station. He had stopped by Uncle Mike's pawn shop for a minute, but now he was already about to walk into the rundown trailer he called home with a happy-go-lucky step. It was an old three-bedroom doublewide. It had green shag carpet on the floor and dark wood paneling on the walls. Heavy orange-yellow curtains hung over the windows, keeping the place darker than it should be, giving it the light of a medieval dungeon. One of the bedrooms was full of junk. Years' worth of stuff that his dad wouldn't throw away, not because he was sentimental, but because he was lazy or too occupied with drinking. Marcus had one bedroom and his dad had the other, which Marcus never entered. It was sloppy; actually, Marcus's bedroom was sloppy, but his dad's was a downright pigsty.

The heavy oak sofa in the living room was covered with orange, yellow, and brown cushions. His dad's recliner was an old La-Z-Boy with worn-out green fabric. There were several well-positioned rips in the cloth from years of repetitive motion. Marcus's dad called it character; Marcus called it crap. There was a black-and-white television sitting on a folding metal TV tray with rabbit-ear antennas pointing to the ceiling.

The heavy odor of cigarettes hung in the air from his father's years of chain smoking. One of two things Marcus's dad had in his hands at all times: a beer, a cigarette, or both. It was hot as usual in the summer because his dad wouldn't get the window unit air conditioner repaired.

A few rotating fans were all they had to circulate air. He didn't see his dad's pick-up truck outside, but with his father it was better safe than sorry, so he announced his entrance.

"Dad, I'm home," he called out.

No one answered. Walking into the kitchen, he opened the fridge, looking for something to eat and possible provisions for the evening on the river with his friends. He poked his head into the cold air and left it there for a minute just to enjoy the lower temperature. He found a slice of cheese and a couple swallows of milk left in the jug. He downed the makeshift lunch and scrounged around for anything else they could use that night. Nothing but beer. Tempting, but he knew his dad would beat him senseless if even one was missing. There had been more than one occasion Marcus took a beating simply because his dad forgot that he was the one who drank all the beer the night before.

"Of course," Marcus complained to himself staring into the barren refrigerator, "we never have nothin' to eat."

Instead of tossing it in the garbage can, he placed the empty milk jug back in the fridge and slammed the door. Opening and closing one cabinet door after another, he struck out in the food department.

"I would starve to death if I didn't have friends," he mumbled.

He was trying to sound sarcastic, but deep down he knew it was true. He probably wouldn't be alive if it weren't for Thad and Rosie. They were the ones who showed him enough love and support, after Tommy died, to help him keep the demons of suicide at bay.

He strolled into his room and flopped down on the bed. Staring up at the ceiling, Marcus didn't want to be the only one to not bring anything. He sat up and looked around his room. Over on the floor, he saw the old canteen that his uncle Mike had given him from the pawnshop. He emptied his school backpack and stuffed the canteen in it. He grabbed his army-surplus flashlight and his AM/FM Panasonic radio, also from his uncle Mike. He put his Swiss Army knife in his pocket and headed for the door.

He made it halfway down the hall before he saw his father standing in the living room. A cigarette in one hand, a beer in the other, of course. Startled, Marcus stopped in his tracks.

"Dad," he said, "I didn't hear you come in."

Marcus's dad took a swallow of beer and stared at his only living son. Wiping the foam from his lips with his forearm, he asked, "Where the hell you going, Marcus?" He was pointing at Marcus's backpack with cigarette in hand.

Marcus looked down at the bag and then back up at his father. "Nowhere, Dad," he answered, "just hanging out with guys at the tree house tonight. We wanna camp out."

"You weren't gonna ask my permission?" his dad asked. Before Marcus could answer, he continued, "You think you run this place? Who the hell you think pays the bills for the shit hole?"

"Dad, I was gonna ask, but when I came home—" Marcus tried to explain before his dad cut him off.

"You don't do a damn thing without asking me first." His dad's voice rose.

Marcus knew what was coming. He'd been here before. It's a terrible thing, a child fighting off his father. No one there to help. No one to get his back. Just him and a belligerent son-of-bitch for a parent. He knew his dad was drunk—hell, he was always drunk—but this time he knew he was angry-drunk. There was a tipping point with him. A mixture of enough alcohol and something to set him off, and all hell would break loose.

Marcus took a step toward his dad, hoping he could slide by before his father lost all control, but that was not going to happen. His dad grabbed him by the collar of his shirt and pushed him into the sofa.

Marcus begged him to stop. "Please, Dad, don't." It was no use. His dad slapped him hard across his face. Marcus tried to dodge the second one, but his dad was too quick. Another slap knocked Marcus to the floor. He tried crawling toward the door, but his dad picked him up by the belt on his jeans.

He threw little Marcus across the living room. The crash into the paneled walls caused picture frames of Tommy to hit the floor. He felt the boot of his dad stomping him in his back more than once. Marcus rolled over and tried returning the kicks as hard and fast as he could. One blow caught his dad in the shin. His dad cussed and grabbed his leg. That was the break Marcus needed. He sprang to his feet, grabbed his backpack, and bolted for the door.

He could hear his dad cussing and yelling as he ran down the dirt road that fronted their rusty trailer. He wasn't crying. He wouldn't give him the pleasure. He knew his father would pass out before long, and by the time Marcus came home the next day, his dad would be halfway sober, apologizing and crying. Saying he's "sorry" and that he needs "help." But it would be only a temporary reprieve. The cycle would start up again soon enough, and Marcus would have to endure another battle with the demon that lived in his house.

Yep, life is a bitch and hope springs eternal.

PHIL'S GRILL

Phil's Grill was hopping when Thad and Marcus arrived. There was a four-man band playing the Allman Brothers and doing a pretty good job, too. The smell of grilled steak laced the air like a poignant invitation. A few couples were dancing near the stage, and the waitresses were working the crowd, milking every nickel they could get in tips. The place felt like it had a pulse. A living, breathing mixture of music, laughter, booze, and incredibly delicious-smelling beef.

"Damn, that smells good," Thad said.

"Hey, there are the girls," Marcus said, pointing to a booth in the corner, in between singing "Lord, I was born a rambling man" and "Trying to make a living and doing the best I can."

Dancing like a redneck on electricity, Marcus made his way to the girls' table; of course they burst out laughing at his epileptic motions. Thad strolled behind Marcus, far enough away where he hoped nobody would think he was with him.

"Ladies, what's up?" Marcus asked with a quirky smile.

"Hi, Allie," Thad said with a grin.

"Well, what am I, chopped onions?" Katey Jo said, looking directly at Thad.

Somewhat put off and definitely surprised at what he saw, Thad mumbled an awkward apology. "I'm sorry, Katey Jo, is that you?"

The last time he saw Katey Jo was a few years after high school. She was a junior at the University of Kansas. She was planning on heading to Alaska to study Eskimos or marine life or the effect the oil pipeline had on migrating caribou, or something to that effect. Back then she was nerd to the max with thick, horn-rimmed glasses, pencil in her hair bun, black pedal pushers with white socks, and a button-down Oxford shirt. But now, well, Thad couldn't believe his eyes. Katey Jo had on a tight, white tank top that she wore obviously bra-less, a plaid miniskirt, black buckle-strap boots up to her knees, and tattoos in numerous places, including a sleeve on her left arm. She wore her jet-black hair in braided pig tails, which gave her a youthful but dangerous look. She still had on nerd glasses, but this time it looked damn sexy instead of geeky.

"Hell yeah, it's me, camera boy," she said braggadociously, "and it's just Kate now."

Marcus slid into the booth next to Katey Jo, and Thad sat next to Allie.

"Well, excuse me, 'just Kate,'" Thad said, laughing.

"Dr. Katey Jo McAnally sounds ridiculous," Kate said. "I mean, who would take me seriously, right?"

The waitress interrupted before Thad could answer. The girls placed their food order, Marcus asked for a burger, and Thad ordered whiskey sours for the ladies and two beers for him and Marcus, along with four shots of Patrón...and whatever it was that "smelled so damn good."

"Doctor?" Thad asked.

"You don't keep up with old classmates, Thaddeus?" Kate asked.

Marcus jumped in. "He doesn't even do Facebook. Just getting him to text is an accomplishment."

"Really?" Allie said smiling at Thad. "You mean I couldn't friend you on Facebook if I wanted to?"

"Uh, yeah, I don't really have time for that social media stuff. Work keeps me hopping," Thad said defensively. "But I know how to e-mail."

"Well, there's that," Kate said, causing the group to laugh.

Marcus looked at Kate and said, "Well, you can call yourself whatever you want, but I'm still calling you KJ."

Kate grabbed Marcus's cheeks and squished them like he was a five-year-old, shaking them back and forth. "You can call me whatever you want, handsome," she said with a big smile.

Marcus was the only one who called her KJ. She liked it, actually; it made her feel special. Kate always had a thing for Marcus. Yeah, he was smaller than most guys she went for. He was irritatingly funny. He didn't keep himself in the best of shape, but still, there was something. She wished they had gotten together in school. Who knows how they would have turned out? Maybe he wouldn't have been divorced. Maybe she would have settled down and had children. Maybe.

Marcus didn't say anything but just grinned ear to ear.

Thad asked Kate again, "Doctor?"

"PhD in marine biology, so it may be KJ to Marcus, but it's Dr. McAnally to you."

They all laughed at the thought. Kate still continued to impress Thad after all these years. The waitress appeared with their drinks, and Marcus helped her hand them out around the table.

"To Rosie," Thad said, raising his shot of Patrón .

The others joined in. "To Rosie," they said in unison, and downed the tequila.

Marcus and Allie both made ugly faces.

"Wow," Allie said.

"That's the good stuff," Marcus added.

"I didn't see you at the funeral Katey Jo—uh…Kate," Thad said.

"I know," she replied. "I know I should've gone. You all know I loved Rosie, but I can't handle funerals. It's stupid and it's selfish, but I can't deal with it. I am going by to see Linda tomorrow. I hope she understands."

Marcus smiled at her. "Aw, she will understand, KJ. Don't worry over it. If you want, I can go with you."

"Thad, order us another round," Kate said. "Come on short stuff," she said to Marcus, "take me to the dance floor and teach me some of those killer moves you've got."

As Marcus led Kate onto the dance floor, Allie and Thad stared at each other for what seemed like ten minutes to Thad. It was only a few seconds, but time distorts through the prism of infatuation.

Thad noticed every little thing about Allie, how she tilted her head back slightly when she laughed, how she circled the top of her whiskey-sour glass with her finger when she was listening intently, how she brushed the side of his leg with her thigh occasionally. He wasn't sure if it was accidental or on purpose, but it felt intense to him either way. He couldn't believe how beautiful she still was, after all these years…perfect.

"Soooo," Allie said, "I hear that camera thing worked out pretty good for you."

The conversation brought Thad back to reality. "Um, yeah, I work at *National Geographic* in DC."

"That's what I hear," she said. "I always knew you would go far with that. You were always so talented."

He wanted to tell her about the picture he took all those years ago, the one of her face with the sunlight in her hair, about how it sat in a frame on his desk, but he thought it might just sound desperate and pathetic. Instead he simply said, "Thanks." He was lost in her eyes when the waitress set more Patrón on the table.

Marcus and Kate stumbled back to the table, laughing, each accusing the other of causing the trip-ups on the dance floor. They piled in the booth as the food and drinks arrived. The four friends drank, ate, and laughed.

"To Rosie," Marcus said, raising his glass in the air.

"To Rosie." The others followed suit.

"Damn, this is fun," Thad said. "Sure wish Rosie was here to chase 'em down with us."

"Remember that time we stole my daddy's whiskey and drank it in the tree house?" Marcus said, laughing with a slight slur to his words. "Rosie got so hammered, he stripped down to his underwear and sang ABBA songs until he passed out. When he woke up the next morning, he was naked, duct-taped to the tree."

"Excellent idea, by the way," Thad said, chuckling.

"Why, thank me very much, my good man," Marcus said in a conceited tone. "He was picking bark out of his ass for a week!"

Everyone laughed out loud at the thought.

"Waitress, more tequila *por favor*," Marcus yelled across the room over the band.

"Slow down there, Marcus," Kate warned.

"What's wrong, KJ? Can't keep up?" Marcus said mockingly.

"You're on, tough guy," Kate answered. "First one to fall off their chair pays for dinner."

Thad and Allie bowed out and left the challenge to the other two.

"Damn good to see you again, Allie," he said.

"Damn good to see you, too, Thaddeus," she said with a smile.

Thad found himself pulled deeper into Allie. It was as if the loud music stopped and the crowd froze, as if the "pulse" disappeared. It was only him and it was only her, just like the first night they started their "adventure" all those years ago…

HOWLING AT THE SKY

The night air was warm and the stars were shinning. From the blackness of the park, Thad swore they looked like bright grains of salt on a dark velvet canvas. Marcus and Rosie were picking on each other as usual. Thad set his trusty Minolta to a thirty-second exposure time and rested the camera on the ground, face up, pointing the lens to the sky, hoping to catch the beauty that his naked eye saw.

After the shutter snapped, Thad sat up and looked at his watch again. He felt a quick pang in his chest as he came to the realization the girls were not going to show. It was already 7:30 and Allie was the one who said 7:00.

He finally said to his friends, "I guess we should get going. Looks like the girls aren't coming."

"What girls aren't coming?" Allie's voice rang out behind him.

"Giving up on us already, Thaddeus?" Katey Jo smirked.

"Hey, guys. Glad you could make it," Thad said, rising to his feet.

"'Bout time," Rosie said, letting go of Marcus's head, which he had firmly locked under his arm.

"Yeah, we could've been there by now," Marcus said.

"Sorry, but we had to work out the details with our parents," Allie said in a defensive tone. "They think we are staying at each other's house tonight, so we had to have everything just right."

Katey Jo piped up. "Yeah, if my dad finds out I'm not at Allie's, all hell's gonna break loose."

All five of her friends immediately looked at Katey Jo.

"What?" she asked.

"We've never heard you cuss before, KJ," Marcus answered.

"Yeah, well, you'd better get damn used to it," Katey Jo responded defiantly. "You've also never seen me sneak out of the house to go camping in the woods with three boys, looking for a dead girl. Have you?"

"True," Thad said, trying to move things along. "Let's check our provisions."

The kids laid their sleeping bags and backpacks on the ground and went through the items.

Thad continued, "I've got two flashlights, my camera with extra rolls of film, a bag of marshmallows, a six pack of Jell-O pudding—"

"What flavor?" Rosie interrupted. "It's not tapioca, is it? I hate tapioca. I tried it one time at the airport when we were stuck there overnight, delayed, waiting for our next flight on our vacation. Dad said it was because of union bastards striking, but I don't know. I just know I barfed up tapioca pudding all over the floor. Man, my dad was pissed—"

Thad finally reciprocated the interruption. "*It's not tapioca*; it's chocolate. I've also got matches."

Rosie shut up, a little embarrassed but otherwise happy it was not tapioca.

"Well, I got a flashlight, batteries, peanut butter crackers, four grape Nehis, a compass and…last month's issue of *Playboy*," Rosie said with a big smile as he lifted the nudie rag up so all could see.

"Ewww," Allie said, "keep that to yourself, please. We brought a bunch of bologna sandwiches, two flashlights, and bag of potato chips."

"Oh, what kind?" Rosie asked, trying to peek into the girl's bag.

"Uh…Lays," Katey Jo said with a "you gotta be kidding" look on her face.

Marcus looked at his friends and said, "Well, I got a flashlight, too, my radio, a canteen of water, and my beautiful smile." He flicked the light on and off under his chin, grinning like a crazy man, and then continued reaching in his pocket. "Oh, and my lucky Swiss Army knife."

"Ok, then," Thad said. "Let's get moving."

The kids picked up their backpacks, and Thad noticed Marcus flinch when he grabbed his.

"Marcus, you ok?" Thad asked with a look of concern.

"Yeah, man," Marcus said, tossing the bag on his back, trying to bunt the question.

Thad prodded a little further. "You sure, man? I saw you wince when you grabbed your bag."

"I'm fine," Marcus said.

Rosie overheard his two friends. Walking up behind Marcus, he grabbed his shoulder to verify the truth in Marcus's answer. Marcus yelped.

"Marcus, what's wrong with your shoulder, man?" Thad asked again.

"Yeah," Allie said, "I noticed you were holding it funny back there."

"Nothing," Marcus answered, slightly annoyed.

Rosie joined in. "Come on, Marcus, let us look at it. Maybe it's something simple."

"It's not simple. It's nothing." Marcus fired back.

Katey Jo looked at Marcus and said, "Don't you think we should see what's wrong with your shoulder? We just want you to be ok, that's all."

Katey Jo seemed to have a connection with Marcus and he with her. He felt his resistance wane, so he dropped the bag. Without saying a word, he lifted up his T-shirt and turned around so his friends could see his back. No one could believe what they saw. Marcus had a bruise the size of a shoebox across his back. His right shoulder was swollen and had red marks in several places.

"Oh my God," Katey Jo said with her hand held to her mouth. "Marcus, what happened?"

Marcus held his head down and said in a barely audible voice, "My dad…he came home while I was packing up my provisions. He had been drinking, and I guess I set him off or something. He threw me against the wall…beat on me some. But I'm tough for a little guy. I will be ok." He tried to muster a smile.

"That son of a bitch," Rosie said.

"I'm sorry, buddy," Thad said. "I shouldn't have pressed you."

"No, it's ok, man," Marcus said.

"I didn't know," Allie said, as if to ask for forgiveness for prying.

"Don't tell anybody, please," Marcus said. "My dad's had it rough. I will be ok."

"Ain't no damn excuse," Rosie said, as if he could get his hands on Marcus's dad.

"Are you gonna be ok, Marcus?" Allie asked.

"Yeah, I'm fine, just a little bruised, see?" He answered, waving his arms back and forth.

"Ok, but if it gets bad you promise me that you will tell me and we will get you seen about," Katey Jo said with a motherly tone.

"Yes, sir, officer sir," Marcus said saluting. "Guys, I'm really fine," he said seriously, "This ain't the first time I've tussled with my dad, and it won't be the last. Now let's get going. Abigail's out there waiting on us."

With that the group gathered up their essentials and started the hike toward the tire swing.

Rosie was out front, trying to act brave. He was the biggest, after all. He felt it was his responsibility to take care of the others, kind of like a bodyguard. It was definitely different hiking there at night than when they performed the same task earlier in the day. Everything that seemed fun and inviting in the sunlight seemed scary and foreboding in the dark. To take his mind off of it, he started whistling the tune from, *The Bridge on the River Kwai*. Marcus walked behind him but close enough to Katey Jo so that he could continually impress her with his wit. At least that's what he told himself. Thad purposefully held back so he could walk next to Allie, but he was careful not to be too obvious.

She was so beautiful. The night stars shined in her blond hair like glitter. Her eyes were so blue they were almost the color of turquoise. She smelled like honeysuckle. When she smiled, Thad swore time slowed down. And she was smiling…at him…it was just Thad and Allie, no one else…

"Sooooo…" Thad began in a drawn-out voice. "It sure is a beautiful night."

"Sure is," Allie responded, looking up at the stars.

"I'm really glad you guys could make it," Thad said, looking down at his feet.

"Me, too," Allie replied. "I just hope my folks don't find out."

"Don't worry. Nobody's gonna say anything to anybody," Thad said in a convincing tone.

Bringing Thad back to reality, Marcus added, "That's right. Nobody's gonna say nothing. We are a pack and a pack looks out for one another."

So much for his not-so-private conversation with Allie. He was mighty glad he didn't say anything too embarrassing. All the same, he turned a light shade of red upon the realization.

Katey Jo looked at Marcus. "A pack? Like a bunch of dogs? You saying I'm a dog, Marcus?" she said in an angry but joking manner.

Allie joined in. "Yeah. You saying we're dogs?" she said, mocking the tone of Katey Jo.

"Uh, no. I ain't saying that," Marcus said with a hint of nervousness.

"Sound like what you said to me," Thad said with a smirk.

Rosie stopped whistling and joined in the verbal attack. "Dogs, Marcus? How insulting."

Marcus tried to stammer out an explanation, but Rosie cut him off with a long howl. Thad, Allie, and Katey Jo quickly joined in. For half a second, Marcus though they were all crazy, but then he gave up and let out a bay that competed well with his friends. Thad quit howling and quickly snapped a photograph of his fellow adventurers howling at the sky. With the flash, they all stopped their canine imitations and looked at Thad. Then a spontaneous eruption of laughter followed suit. Rosie restarted his marching tune and the group joined in, following the winding path onward toward their final destination for the night. Marcus's shoulder was feeling much better. It's funny how levity can mend a wound.

The old tire swing awaited their arrival patiently. Its riverbank guarded its secrets like a child trying to hide the contents of a gift just given to a parent at Christmas, likely to spill the beans before the wrapping can even be removed. There was more to reveal about Abigail Lowery, and it was past time to spill the beans.

GOOD-NIGHT KISS

The band was on its last set. The food was gone, the candle on the table had burned out, and Marcus was wobbling like an old man on a rubber crutch. Thad thought it best to wind down the evening, so he asked for the tab.

"Here, let me get that," Kate said, opening up Marcus's wallet.

"A doctor and a pick-pocket," Thad said, laughing at Kate.

They settled the bill and made their way out the door. Thad could not help but notice how beautiful Allie was when she left a room. Her long hair swaying with her confident yet feminine walk. He just stood and watched and smiled. Noticing she left her purse in the chair, he grabbed it and rushed to catch up with her.

"You leaving this behind, so I would find it and bring it to you tomorrow?" Thad asked Allie with a sly grin. "Very sneaky, Miss Thompson."

Seeing the purse in Thad's hand, Allie grabbed it with a surprised laugh. "You got me," she said.

They both laughed and just enjoyed the moment together.

"I had a good time tonight, Thad," Allie said as he walked her to her car.

"Me, too," he replied.

Why do I still act like a kid? he thought.

Here he was, a full-grown man…a successful full-grown man, and next to Allie Thompson he could muster up no more to say than a corny joke and a "me, too." It wasn't like he hadn't had other lovers in his life. There was Celia in college, who for two years made it hard for him to study journalism. There was the airline stewardess who managed to be on more than one of his overseas flights. He'd even been engaged once before. Melissa Jenkins was a strong, beautiful journalist. They shared the same passion for their careers and for life. They both thought marriage was the next logical step in their relationship. But Thad knew in the end, it takes more than common interest and fun…it takes true love. True friendship does not a marriage make. They were still friends to this day, but the wedding never happened.

But then there was Allie. His heart never left her hands, and he knew it. His first true love. Part of him felt guilty that he was even thinking about this on the day he buried his best friend. Part of him felt guilty that he let her get away all those years ago. After high school, she went to the University of Colorado in Boulder. He headed south to the University of Oklahoma. They promised to call and write. They promised to be true. They promised all the right things, but the farther the distance, the shorter the relationship, and eventually Allie told him in a letter that she needed to move on. He knew it was the right thing to do, but he always thought they would be together forever. He rationalized that if they couldn't make it apart for a few years and seven hundred miles from each other, then they couldn't make it together for a lifetime. Still, she was "the one," and no one ever really took her place.

"God, Rosie would've loved this tonight," Allie said, looking up at the stars.

It's funny how looking up at the sky seems to improve communication with the dead.

"Yes, he would," Thad replied. He sighed deeply and continued, "I miss him already, Allie. I mean, I just don't get it. Why Rosie? He's the only one of us with a family. He had his shit together. I've been shot at, hung off a cliff, kidnapped, and held for ransom. It should've been me to go first. I wasn't planning on burying my best friend. He was supposed to bury me. Some drunk idiot with a key changes fate."

"Maybe 'some idiot with a key' was fate," Allie said. "We don't know how much time we have, Thad. Today, tomorrow, next year, nobody knows. If it's meant to be, it's meant to be."

Thad thought on that for a moment.

Allie continued, "That's why if you have a chance at something great, you need to grab it."

They stood face-to-face, staring into each other's eyes. Thad could feel her warm breath. He could smell her perfume, and it pulled him into her.

"You know the cool thing about tattoos, KJ?" Marcus said drunkenly as he and Kate swaggered toward his truck parked next to Allie's car. "They let people know you are who you are, and you are someone you loves tattoos!"

Thad and Allie quickly stepped apart upon hearing their friends approach.

"Wow, that is so...profound, Marcus," Kate said.

"Well, I'm a profound kinda guy," Marcus said. "Profound Marcus Pawley, the proprietor of Pawley's Pawn and Purchase. Hey, say that three times fast. Profound Pawley proliferer of Paw Paws Pawley Purchase...Damn that's hard!"

"Come on, Marcus, let's get you in the truck," Kate said.

She was propping him up, holding his arm around her shoulders. She was still taller than him—even more so with her boots on—though he grew a good six inches through high school. He had to look up to talk to her when they were both standing.

"How come you aren't drunkened up as I did?" Marcus fumbled the errant words. "I saw you drink as many shh—shoooooooters as me."

"Years in the cold of Alaska," she answered, "you drink a lot to stay warm. Tolerance is both a bitch and a blessing."

With that, Thad stepped around to take Marcus's other arm, and they eased him into the passenger seat of his truck. Kate reached in his jeans pocket and groped around for the keys to give to Thad.

"Hey, I'm not that kinda guy!" Marcus said, smiling from ear to ear. "You gotta at least take me out to dinner first…Oh wait…you just did. Ok, KJ, knock yourself out, but be careful. He bites. Ha ha…"

"Not as hard as I do," Kate said. "Thanks for buying supper!"

She laughed, gave him a quick kiss on the lips, and tossed the keys to Thad. She closed the door and walked over to Allie's Ford Mustang. "Toss me the keys," she said to Allie, who complied.

Opening the passenger door, she sat halfway down before looking at Allie and saying, "Would you kiss the guy already? Jeez, you two…" She slammed the door and turned on the car radio.

"Ha ha," Thad stammered out a whimper of a laugh.

"I have really missed you Thad," Allie said. "I wanted to call you and just talk when I was going through my divorce, but I didn't want to come across as rebounding, ya know?"

"I've missed you, too," Thad said. "It's been so long, Allie, I figured I never crossed your mind."

"Thaddeus," she said looking deep into his eyes, "not a day goes by that you don't cross my mind…or a night, for that matter."

She smiled a seductive smile and softly kissed him. There it was again, frozen time. Nothing moved, nothing made a sound, nothing. She slid behind the wheel and told him she would call him tomorrow. He just stood there smiling, like a dumb fourteen-year-old kid, watching her tail lights fade into the darkness.

"Hey," Marcus called out from the truck. "What gets vomit out of carpet?"

Thad opened the driver's side door to Marcus's F150 and took a step back.

"Jesus, Marcus," he said with empathetic disgust. "Let's get you home buddy."

ONE MORE BEER

T had pulled up to the cemetery behind the little brownstone church, aiming his high beams at Rosie's grave and leaving the engine running in park. He grabbed the six-pack he picked up at the all-night corner store when he dropped Marcus off. "Dropped" was not the right word; "carried" was better. *Good thing Marcus was a featherweight,* he thought. He left him in his boxers, tucked in bed, nice and tight.

"The things I do for my friends," he said as he cleaned Marcus's dinner out of the floorboard. He kept his truck for the night and planned on swapping it with him in the morning.

Thad wanted to come see Rosie alone. He had lost one parent and all of his grandparents, and as bad as that was, it was the way of things. Nature running its course. It still hurt and he still missed them all, but there was something more poignant in losing someone before his time. It cuts a little deeper. Maybe because your mind is not prepared for it. Maybe it reminds you of your own mortality. Maybe it just isn't fair. Whatever it was, Thad had never hurt like this. Not even when he and Allie broke up all those years ago. It was like a part of him was gone, and he wanted—no, he needed—to come down here and sit with his best friend. It did not matter the hour; it only mattered the reason. And the reason was Thad missed his friend more than anything.

Graveyards were usually spooky at night, but when have you just put your best friend in one, they feel more like a campout. He walked to the grave. He could smell the dirt, which was fresh and clean. He sat down and placed the six-pack on the ground, choosing two cans to open.

"Rosie, we had a great time tonight, buddy," he said to the darkness. "We all went out to eat and to raise a few to you. You should've seen Marcus. He got into a drinking contest with Katey Jo—oh, she goes by Kate now, Dr. McAnally to me," he chuckled at that. "Marcus danced around like a mongoose in a mine field. He got so drunk Kate had to carry him out of the bar, and I had to drive him home. Took me thirty minutes to clean the puke out of his truck." Thad laughed and wiped a small tear that began to form in his eye. He took a drink of ale out of one can and poured some onto the fresh dirt out of the other. "I brought you a beer, your favorite, Budweiser…king of the beers. Kind of like you, amigo, king of the world. There wasn't a thing you couldn't do if you set your mind to it…except math." That made Thad laugh out loud. He took another swig and poured more for Rosie.

"Jesus, we missed you tonight, brother. I missed you tonight." The tears began flowing a little easier. This time he did not try to clear his throat. "Rosie, I don't know what to do without you here, man. I've got so much left I want to talk to you about. I'm planning on getting married one day, having kids, all that shit. I just hope I'm half the father you were."

Thad did not even try to dry his eyes. "Linda and the kids are doing good. Don't you ever worry about them buddy. I will be there. Your boys are strong and good. Damn if that Paulie doesn't look just like you, God help him." Thad had a mixture of laughter and tears. They shared another swallow, and he looked up at the stars.

"Allie is," he said, pausing, "Allie is…I don't know what Allie is. She is so beautiful, Rosie. If you could tell me, you'd say something like, 'Quit being a jackass and go get her.' The thing is, I love her, buddy. I never stopped loving her. I want to go over there right now and tell her, but I don't know how to make it work. I guess sometimes you just gotta step back and take it all in. Life is short, ya know." Thad laughed. "Look who I'm telling"

"It's never gonna be the same without you Rosie," Thad said with his head down. "All those crazy damn summers, the tree house, football games—'Marcus, go long.'" He made a motion like he was throwing a touchdown pass. "All those apple tarts, that old tire swing, the Cottonwood. We had it all back then, partner, we had it all...I'm never gonna forget...I'm never gonna forget you, brother." He let out a long breath. "Say hi to my dad for me and Tommy. Oh, and if you run into Granddad, tell him that photo thing worked out ok. Rest well, my friend."

Thad dried his tears and stood up. He poured the rest of Rosie's beer onto the grave and walked back to the truck.

He looked up at the heavens through the Ford's windshield. "God, you take care of my brother. He's a big guy, acts tough and all, but he needs someone to talk to on occasion...oh, and don't let him con you into streaking down those streets of gold." He turned the keys and Marcus's old F150 roared to life. He backed out of the cemetery and made his way back to his mother's house.

MARSHMALLOWS AND GHOST STORIES

Rosie was in the lead as they made their way through the dark woods, nearing their destination. Passing the water treatment facility, Rosie knew they were close to the swollen creek they had crossed earlier. He slowed his pace until he reached the engorged stream. Flashing his beam of light back and forth, he looked for the fallen tree they used as a bridge.

"There it is," Rosie said, spying the pine.

The kids lined up one at a time to cross the water. Marcus went first. It was much more difficult in the dark, that was for sure. Still, he nimbly made his way to the other side. Thad helped Allie on to the tree and told Marcus to grab her as she came across. Allie slowly walked across but showed no signs of lack of balance. She crossed easily, as did Katey Jo.

"I'll go next," Thad told Rosie. He carefully slid his feet across the thin tree. He was halfway across when the tree rolled ever so slightly. Waving his hands in a circular motion in an attempt to regain his balance, Thad began to correct the problem. Rosie thought his buddy was about to go into the water, so instinctively, he jumped on the tree and grabbed Thad's hand to help steady him. It did not have the desired effect. Both boys began flailing their arms wildly and the tree began rocking back and forth. It finally gave in to the excess weight, and both boys went crashing into the creek, still holding hands.

Thad heard Allie scream, "Thad!" right before he went under.

The water was deep enough to fully submerge the two but not wide enough to carry them away. They both grabbed hold of the embankment and crawled out of the muddy water. Soaked to the bone, Thad looked at Rosie.

"What were you doing?" Thad asked, obviously upset.

"I was trying to save your ass from falling," Rosie said. "A 'thanks' would be nice."

"I had it under control, man," Thad said. "You soaked us!"

"It looked like you were about to fall," Rosie argued.

"I wasn't gonna fall," Thad said, "until you grabbed me."

"That's the last time I try to help you, ungrateful..." Rosie's words trailed off as he sloshed off toward the tire swing.

Thad felt bad. He knew Rosie was trying to help him; he was just embarrassed in front of Allie. He got his soggy self up and the rest of the group headed toward Rosie. They heard the sound of the river just up ahead. Walking through the last bit of underbrush, Rosie saw the tire hanging from the tree limb. It was only earlier that same day they had tied it back on to the tree.

"We're here," Rosie said.

"And we're queer!" Marcus said.

"Ha ha. Very funny," Allie said in a condescending voice.

Marcus fired back. "You guys gotta lighten up."

"He's right," Thad said, shivering. "That's the only way to stand him for very long."

Marcus answered with a "ha ha ha."

Looking at her two wet friends, Katey Jo said, "We need to call it quits. Get you two back home."

"No way," Rosie barked through chattering teeth. "We've been walking for like an hour, and I'm starving."

"We don't quit," Thad said. He tried to act determined, but actually he just didn't want his night with Allie to end so soon.

"Well, you two are soaked," Katey Jo said. "If we're gonna stay, we need to start a fire, get you out of your clothes, and hang them up to dry."

"What? No way," Rosie said, shaking almost violently.

"We'll be all right," Thad said through his clacking teeth.

"Sure you will," Katey Jo said. "You both will die from hypothermia if you stay wet. It's supposed to get down to the fifties tonight. Either you two get out of those clothes, or I'm going home and telling."

"But…but you're girls," Rosie said like an embarrassed five-year-old.

"She's right," Allie said. "You need to get out of those clothes. You can go behind the bushes and give them to Marcus. We will get a fire going. You can get into your sleeping bags and nobody will see anything. If you don't, I am going home right now."

Reluctantly the two waterlogged friends agreed and shuffled off behind the bushes.

Taking off their wet rags, Rosie muttered, "Now I know why mom always said wear clean underwear."

Both he and Thad laughed and called for Marcus to come gather their soggy clothes. He brought them their sleeping bags and the two boys zipped their naked bodies inside the warm blankets. They hopped like rabbits back toward the others. Both girls broke out into laughter at the sight of the boys bouncing in a sleeping bag.

"Looks like a potato-sack race!" Katey Jo said through her laughter.

Marcus gathered some wood and formed a good tee-pee shape. He added a few well-placed pine cones and a match, and before long they had a nice campfire. That year as a Cub Scout came in handy for something. They hung the wet clothes on sticks and stuck them in the ground near the fire.

Sitting close to the campfire, Rosie and Thad were quickly warming, prodding Rosie to claim he was still starving.

"We have bologna sandwiches, pudding, marshmallows," Allie said.

"Ooh, marshmallows," Rosie said with excitement.

"What are you, four?" Katey asked Rosie.

"I'm fourteen and I'm wet and I want marshmallows," Rosie said in a defiant voice. "Is that a problem?"

"Marshmallows it is," Katey Jo said, cutting her eyes at Allie.

The kids tore into the bag of Kraft marshmallows and stuck the treats on the end of sticks.

Holding his over the fire until it turned black, Marcus spoke up. "You know what goes good with toasted marshmallows?" he asked.

"Graham crackers!" Rosie said a little too emphatically.

"No. Well, true," Marcus said, "but I'm talking about ghost stories!"

"Yeah, ghost stories," Thad added.

Thad was hoping it would make Allie want to sit even closer to him. He had already chosen a place around the campfire next to her.

"Ohhhh, I like ghost stories," Allie said.

Perfect, Thad thought.

Katey Jo said, "I'll start." She cleared her throat and began in a low, whispered voice. "There is this legend. It's about a group of kids, an old man, and a dog. Right here near this very spot. The creek that these two knuckleheads fell in, actually, is where the legend started. What we affectionately call 'Crap Creek' went by another name long ago…'Murder Creek.'"

The fire crackled and the cool wind gently blew.

Katey Jo continued, "Fifty years ago there was a crazy old man that lived in a little shack near the creek. He would come into town about once a week on his bike, the kind with a basket in the front. He would buy provisions and whatnot. Everyone called him Booker. Well, see, Booker wouldn't talk to anyone. Never said a word. Most folks thought he couldn't even speak. He had an old hound dog that ran alongside his bike. The faithful dog would always wait outside the store next to Booker's bike while he went in to buy his goods. One day a group of teenagers, three boys and two girls just like us, were hanging around the store when they saw Booker and his dog pull up. Now these kids were mean, no-good troublemakers. They started picking on Booker's hound. They were poking at him with sticks, taunting him, even kicking him. The dog tried to stand his ground, yelping and howling every time one of the hooligans would hit him. He backed into the street growling while the kids kept up their taunting. Booker heard the commotion and came running outside, but it was too late. Just then, a car came racing down the street and hit the dog, killing him. Booker dropped to his knees and cried as he held the poor dog in his arms. All the while, the kids just laughed at him."

Katey Jo looked around the fire at the silent faces of her friends. She knew she had them hooked. She waited before she continued, letting the suspense build.

"At that moment Booker looked up at the teenagers and spoke the first words anyone had ever heard him say. *'Murder...murder!'* The kids laughed at Booker and went on their way, leaving the old man in the street with his poor dog. The very next night one of the kids was found dead in her bed. No apparent cause, just dead. The next day, another kid was found dead. Same thing the next two days, two more kids were found dead. Then there was only one left. This kid was some kind of scared; he knew Booker was behind the deaths somehow. So he decided he wasn't going to wait for old man Booker to kill him. He was going to go find him in his shack and stick a knife in his throat."

Katey Jo stared at her marshmallow in the fire, slowly turning it, almost enjoying watching the flesh of the thing melt away.

"The last teenager crept into the woods that night, rusty old butcher knife in his hand. Quiet as a mouse, he crept. Closer, closer to the shack. He peeked through the window and saw old man Booker rocking back and forth in his chair, staring wildly into the fire. Ready to do the deed, the boy slowly, quietly opened the door and snuck into the rusty old shack. As he raised the knife to pierce Booker's neck, he heard a rattling behind him. Startled, he looked back to see his friends faces, trapped in mason jars, screaming for help but no words coming out of their mouths.

"'How…what…' the boy said. He turned back to see old man Booker standing right in front of him. Except he was larger than before and his eyes were burning with fire.

"'Their souls are mine forever and now yours is, too.' The boy tried to scream, but Booker sucked his soul right out of his mouth. The boy's body fell limp to the ground. Booker opened a new mason jar and blew the young soul into it, capping it tight. He gathered up all five jars and threw them into the creek when it was high, just like tonight. He laughed as he watched the kids' faces begging for help as they floated away.

"They say on a moonless night, like tonight, you can hear the screams of five teenage kids and the baying of a hound…and the laughing of an old man. Listen…listen…*Boo!*"

All fours kids screamed at the same time and then burst into laughter.

"Holy shit, KJ," Marcus said. "I nearly peed myself."

"Wow, Katey Jo," Rosie said, surprised. "I mean…wow!"

There is a fine line between fear and laughter. Both stimulate the senses, both release endorphins, both create emotion, both bring you closer together. Fear just digs in a little deeper.

The fire was getting to a decent size, warming the faces of the kids as they ate bologna sandwiches and browned marshmallows on sticks. The kids sat around the flames, not saying anything for a minute or two. They just watched them flicker, almost hypnotizing each and every one.

Finally Marcus broke the silence. "That's just a ghost story." His eyes never left the flames. "Abigail Lowery is a real-life horror story."

No one said anything, waiting to hear what Marcus had to say.

Marcus continued, "I went by Uncle Mike's again today. He told me about the real stuff that happened to all those girls the Cottonwood Killer murdered. Stuff the papers wouldn't print. He said that some of the girls' faces were painted like clowns. Except the smile wasn't a lipstick smile; it was a smile from ear to ear made with a knife. He would cut them from the corners of the mouths, slice them wide open while they were alive. One girl had all of her fingers cut off on one hand and on the other her fingers were sewed together like a mitt. One girl's face was peeled completely off. Another one—"

"That's enough, Marcus," Allie said. "We get it. He was a sick bastard."

"Sorry, Allie. Didn't mean to upset you," Marcus said. "Just thought I would let you guys know what he might have done to Abigail."

"It's sad that she doesn't have a proper grave, you guys," Thad said. "If we find her, we need to make sure that she gets one."

"Definitely," Rosie said. He raised his flaming marshmallow to the sky and declared, "To Abigail Lowery, if I find you, I promise to get you buried proper."

One by one, the others in the group raised their sticks to the sky and declared, "I promise."

The Cottonwood River swished by in a rhythmic cadence as embers danced through the trees from the fire below. If they had listened closer, they could have almost heard the faint whisper of a young girl, crying in the night, begging for help. The pops and crackles of the fire seemed to be telling their own stories.

KATEY JO VS. KATE

The sun was especially bright this morning; at least Kate thought so. It may have had something to do with the battle of Patrón she engaged in with Marcus the night before. She stood on the front porch and instantly saw Rosie's imprint on the structure. Rustic wood siding, dark green shutters, well kept and clean, all so Rosie. Even the Kansas City Chiefs banner hanging by the door. Especially the Kansas City Chiefs banner. She chuckled under her breath at the football memorabilia.

She was not embarrassed by her tattoos, in fact, she was proud of them. Still there were times when it was best to keep them covered. Telling a good friend's wife you are sorry for her loss is one of those times. She wore her hair straight today and toned down her outfit significantly. She had on a long-sleeved white blouse and navy blue skirt with heels. She looked the exact opposite of the woman she was the night before. She wasn't a hypocrite. She was just respectful.

A wind chime played its song as a gentle breeze crawled across the porch. The grass was a deep shade of green. You could tell Rosie took good care of it. There was an old swing set standing on the front lawn looking like it was patiently waiting for an enthusiastic child to come out and play. It looked like it might have to wait awhile.

She wasn't totally hung over from drinking last night, but she wasn't exactly ship-shape, either. She chuckled again, thinking about Marcus and wondering how bad he had it this morning. *Lightweight,* she thought to herself and smiled. She straightened her blouse and knocked on the heavy oak door.

When the door opened, Kate looked down at a young boy, probably no more than four years old…the spitting image of Rosie. He did not say a word but just held on to the doorknob looking up at her, so she opened the conversation.

"Hello, there," Kate said with a tone that was meant for a child. "I'm Kate, a good friend of your dad's. Is your mom home?"

"My dad is dead," the child said, obviously saddened.

"Oh, I know. I am so sorry," Kate replied.

"Paulie, who is there?" Kate heard a woman's voice coming from inside the house.

The woman walked to the door and took over for Paulie.

"Hello," she said, "can I help you?"

Kate did not recognize her but figured she was part of Linda's family.

"Yes," Kate answered. "I'm Kate McAnally, a good friend of Rosie's. I just wanted to pay my respects to Linda."

"Of course," the woman said. "I'm Teresa, Linda's sister. Won't you please come in?"

Teresa held the door open and motioned for Kate to enter. She closed the door behind her and asked for Kate to wait while she retrieved Linda. Once again Kate could see Rosie everywhere, in the pictures on the mantle, in the colors of the walls, in the recliner where he obviously sat, and definitely in the eyes of the little man, Paulie, who opened the door. She walked over to the mantle where one picture in particular caught her attention. It was Rosie, Thad, Marcus, Allie, and her, all together by the old tire swing. She remembered Thad taking that picture on the night they looked for Abigail. It made her smile. She placed the picture back on the mantel and walked to the sofa. Standing in the living room, she noticed the amount of casseroles, pies, and various other foods on the dining room table. The thought of food made her a little nauseous.

Maybe I'm losing my touch a little bit, she thought. She placed her hand to her mouth wondering if Marcus was worse.

"Katey Jo," Linda said with her arms open wide as she entered the living room, "it's so good to see you."

Kate did not have the heart to tell her it was "Kate" now, so she simply hugged her.

"I am so sorry about Rosie," Kate said, still hugging Linda. "I couldn't believe it."

"I know," Linda said, "I still can't. Please have a seat. Can I get you something to eat?"

The thought did not sit well in Kate's stomach. "No, thank you," she answered, "but I would love a cup of coffee."

Teresa overheard from the kitchen and stuck her head around the corner. "I'll get it," she said. "How do you take it?"

"Black will be fine," Kate answered. Turning to Linda, she said, "I am so sorry I did not make it to the funeral yesterday."

She wanted to tell her the truth—that she couldn't handle funerals—but she did not want to sound petty, so she left it at that.

"Oh, that's ok, Katey Jo," Linda said. "Rosie knew how much you loved him. He missed you over the years. He used to tell me all the time how much 'the gang' meant to him and how he wanted to get all of you together again. It's sad that it takes a funeral to do it." She looked down at her hands.

Kate felt bad that she hadn't been home in so long, that she hadn't kept up with her good friends like she should have. Linda could tell the thought made her uncomfortable, so she continued, "I'm sorry, Katey Jo. I didn't mean it like it sounded. He loved you a lot…he loved all of you a lot."

Teresa brought out her coffee. Kate thanked her and took a sip. The warm dark beverage felt good going down her throat. It took the edge off the hangover that was steadily revving up its engines.

As Linda continued to reminisce over Rosie's time spent with his friends, Kate thought of all the years she had been away from Emporia. After high school she studied at the University of Kansas, where she received her bachelor of science in biology. She graduated cum laude and then headed to the University of Alaska where she received her doctorate in marine biology. It was a given that Kate would be well educated just as Thad would be a world-class photographer. Some people have their destinies almost laid out for them like a highway. All they have to do is follow the path to reach their destination.

Although the University of Kansas was only a couple of hours from Emporia, she wrapped herself so much in her studies that she rarely ventured off campus. At least that is what she did for the first three years of college. The last year she had a breakdown of sorts, although she preferred to call it a breakthrough.

One night, studying for yet another exam, her roommate crashed in with a group of friends. Kate argued that she couldn't concentrate with a party going on. Her roommate told her all she did was study and she needed to learn to live a little. Kate accused her roommate of being a slacker. Name calling was the next logical step. One thing lead to another and pushing and shoving occurred. The squabble spilled into the hall and eventually out of the dorm where hair pulling and slapping began. The campus police had to separate the girls and lock them in "college jail" for the night.

Kate was humiliated. She was never a troublemaker. She was a Goody Two-shoes…and that's when it hit her. Her roommate was right. She had let life slide by with her nose in a book. She was as straight-laced as they came. She never partied, never let her hair down, never even had a boyfriend. Hell, she was a twenty-two-year-old virgin. The thought depressed her.

She took the exam the next day, fully unprepared and expecting to fail. To her surprise, she aced it. It was if a light turned on in her head. She had an epiphany. Living life and expanding your mind did not have to be mutually exclusive. In fact, they were codependent. You could not have one without the other. That night she apologized to her roommate and asked for her help to create a new Katey Jo. Her roommate told her the first thing they had to do would be to stop calling her "Katey Jo."

"From now on we will call you 'Kate,'" her roommate said. And so Kate was born, or reborn to be more precise.

She blossomed like a flower, like an oleander, beautiful and dangerous. Drinking, boys, parties, risk-taking, tattoos…you name it and Kate did it. When someone is deprived of nutrients for a long period of time, given the chance, they will devour whatever food is presented to them. Well, Katey Jo was deprived, and Kate devoured.

She still maintained an A+ average, which was remarkable. But the party and stress of school had its price. Katey Jo paid the toll for Kate's highway to hell. She woke up one morning with no clue where she was or how she got there. Her clothes were torn, she was sick to her stomach, and she was bleeding. She could not remember or be sure, but she had a feeling that she had been raped. The last thing she remembered was partying at a friend's house and talking to a hot guy. He was smart, he was cool, and he was available. But that's all she remembered. She would have nightmares of someone raping her, and she would wake up crying. But she had no real evidence and felt ashamed, so she locked it away with all her other transgressions and went about her business as though nothing happened.

It hardened Kate, but it also made her wiser. No longer was she going to be the party animal that she had become, but no way in hell was she going back to Katey Jo. So Kate struck a balance, somewhere between book nerd and party girl. She likes to call herself a party nerd. All books and no play made Katey Jo a dull girl; however all play and no books made Kate a dead girl. She did keep the name Kate. She liked it.

The University of Alaska welcomed her eagerly, and she did not disappoint. She tore through her doctorate studies and earned her degree early. She loved marine biology. She loved the ocean and Alaska. Strange for a Kansas girl to love the cold, the very cold, but it suited her. She made Alaska her home. Men wove through her life like a harlequin tapestry, but no one ever stole her heart. She told herself it was better that way. She was a beautiful woman—tall, sexy, and a bit dangerous. Getting a man was easy; keeping him was another thing. But she was gone a lot anyway, so she took it as it came. And she was ok with that.

Looking around Linda's room, though, she felt that part of her longed for what Rosie had, a spouse, children, all the parts of a "normal" life. She thought of Marcus, always a good friend but nothing romantic. Maybe she could get him to visit her in Alaska one day. And who knew what could happen? But the fact was, he was her good friend who had a life in Kansas, and she was a loner who spent half her time in the ocean and the other half in the cold winters of Alaska.

"Katey Jo…Katey Jo, are you ok?" Linda's question snapped her back into the moment.

"Yes, I'm sorry," she answered, embarrassed. "I'm just a little under the weather." She stood up and said, "I'll let you go. Once again, I'm sorry I missed the funeral. I heard it was beautiful. If I can do anything for you, please call me."

She hugged Linda and made her way out of the house. Little Paulie was holding his aunt Teresa's hand by the front door.

"My daddy's dead," he said one last time. This time Kate did not reply, she simply smiled at the familiar eyes looking up at her. She caressed his face with her hand and turned to go outside. She stopped at her car and looked back one last time. "Goodbye, Rosie," she whispered.

FREEBIRDS

The clothes were nearly dry, so Rosie and Thad decided it was time to get out of their sleeping bags and back into more normal apparel. They hopped behind the bushes and waited for Marcus to bring them their drier yet smoky outfits.

"Here ya go," Marcus said, walking around the bushes with clothes in hand, "freshly roasted jeans, baked shirts, and toasted underwear."

Rosie grabbed the clothes and Marcus headed back to the fire.

As the boys sorted out their effects, Thad spoke up,. "Sorry I yelled at you earlier. I know you were trying to help. I was just embarrassed, is all."

"Dude, you don't have to apologize. I ain't gonna let anything happen to you," Rosie said, smiling at his buddy.

Just like a big guy would do, Rosie grabbed his friend and hugged him.

That's how Marcus found them, behind the bushes...in their underwear...hugging.

"Ahem," Marcus said, clearing his throat. "Am I interrupting something?"

Thad and Rosie pushed each other away.

"Hey! We're getting dressed here," Thad shouted.

"Not cool, Marcus," Rosie said. "He was just thanking me for helping him on the old tree bridge."

"Yeah. I was just thanking him for trying to help me on the old tree bridge, that's all," Thad said, pulling his jeans up.

"What about me?" Marcus said. "I tried to help. Don't I get a hug?"

"I'll hug your ass…like a grizzly bear," Rosie said, charging at Marcus. Realizing he was still without pants, he turned back behind the bushes like a squirrel darting out in front of a car on the highway.

Marcus laughed and headed to join the girls, barely able to contain himself as he told them what he just saw. Rosie finished dressing and returned to the campfire with the others. Thad was right behind him when he saw the faint purple petal of a wildflower. He shined his flashlight on it and thought it was something Allie would like. He picked the flower and ran back to the campfire.

"Guys, show us where you found the necklace," Allie said when the boys rejoined them.

"Over there by that tree branch in the water," Rosie said, walking to the fallen limb while adjusting his shirt.

They walked over to the edge of the riverbank. Shining their flashlights into the murky, churning water.

"It was caught right here," Rosie said, pointing.

Seeing an opportunity to snuggle by the fire with Allie for the night, Thad spoke up, "Well, it's too dark right now to look, so let's search around here early in the morning and see what else we can find."

Everyone agreed, so they all sat around the fire, waiting for exhaustion to either leave their bodies or take over completely.

Katey Jo was talking about the upcoming school year. Rosie was talking about how high the river was. Marcus was talking about that new movie *Jaws*. And Thad...well, he sat next to Allie, saying nothing. He was trying to muster up the nerve to give her the flower he had picked. Part of him was saying "Just do it," another part was saying "You'll look stupid." He stared at the fire silently. Finally he let his "Just do it" side take over, and he went for it.

"I got something for you," he said, handing the freshly picked wild-flower to Allie.

Surprised, Allie said, "It's beautiful, Thad." She inhaled the sweet aroma with a long deep breath. "Wildflowers are my favorite. Where did you find it?"

"Behind the bushes over there," Thad said, pointing to where he and Rosie got dressed. "I saw it and thought it was beautiful..." He paused and thought, *Come on, just do it.* He looked her in the eyes and said, "Just like you."

He couldn't believe he just said that. He had actually told Allie Thompson, the prettiest girl in school, that she was beautiful. His elation was quick lived, however. His mind instantly began asking, *What if she doesn't say anything? What if she laughs? Or worse, what if she says, "Ohhh, gross"?*

But Allie, looking back at him, said one thing: "Thad." She put the flower behind her ear, smiled, and kissed him on his cheek.

Thad reached for his camera and pointed it at Allie. "Smile," he said. She looked at him as the flash went off, and they both laughed.

Listening to Marcus explain to Rosie how a giant man-eating shark could terrorize an entire town, Katey Jo caught a glimpse of Thad's flash. "Hey, take our picture," she said.

"Yeah, get a group shot," Rosie said.

"Where did you get that wild prairie rose?" Katey Jo asked, pointing to the flower in Allie's hair. Katey Jo was indeed a very smart girl, and very observant.

Thad quickly diverted Katey Jo's question by telling everyone to stand up before Allie could answer. He gathered everyone together and surveyed the area for the best possible shot. He had to take in to account the darkness of the night, the glow of the campfire, and their surroundings. There was so much more that went into a good picture besides point and shoot. Settling on his choices, he set his camera to a fifteen-second timer and placed it on a rock nearby. All five kids stood together and waited for the shutter to release. It flashed. *Another moment in time*, Thad thought.

He sat back down next to Allie and was staring into the fire when he felt her fingers brush ever so slightly on his hands. It was like electricity wrapped in cotton candy. There it was again, another brush. He couldn't believe Allie Thompson was trying to hold his hand. No matter what happened to him the rest of his entire life, this moment would go down as the best ever.

Allie Thompson wants to hold my hand, he thought, trying to keep a cool, nonchalant look on his face.

He reciprocated and slowly let her soft fingers intertwine with his.

Perfect fit, he thought.

She was so soft, almost like cream. Neither one said anything for the longest time. They sat there, staring into the fire, holding each other's hands. As far as Thad was concerned, that was good enough for him. Everything else might come and go, but they could just stay right here and hold hands forever.

But then he felt a sudden urge. Not wanting to let her go, he tried to hold it. The eventual squirm started. He moved a little left, then a little right. It was getting painfully obvious that he was going to either pee all over himself and lose her hand forever or let her hand go for a minute and keep his pride intact. He chose the latter.

"I'll be right back," he said.

"Gotta pee?" she asked with a smile. "I noticed your dance moves."

"My dance moves?" he said, embarrassed.

"Yeah," she said, "the pee-pee dance. Ha ha—"

Marcus, eavesdropping on their conversation, interrupted. "You should see my dance moves!"

With that he switched on his Panasonic portable AM/FM radio and jumped up ecstatically when he heard the intro to "Freebird" by Lynyrd Skynyrd.

"Guys! I *love* this song!" Marcus shouted to the night sky.

He turned up the volume to the max. Grabbing his 1960 Les Paul air guitar, he cranked out the licks like Allen Collins himself and began shaking his head up and down perfectly out of sync with his hips gyrating right to left. It was like two monkeys fighting in a bag, but it was an awesome sight.

It didn't take long before Rosie joined in, letting his vocal chops fly *free as a bird.*

Katey Jo looked at Allie and then up they came, dancing like no one was watching. Thad started laughing so hard his bladder reminded him quickly that it was still there, so he headed for the nearest bush and felt the sweet release of nature's call. He returned just in time to see his friends break into the freakishly long guitar solo. He joined in the mayhem. Every one of them playing their air guitars to the melody. As the song faded, Frankie Valli filled the airwaves with "My Eyes Adored You."

Katey Jo grabbed Marcus by the hand and said, "Come on, Fred Astaire, let's show them how to do it."

The two of them slid into the slow tempo and glided to the music, Marcus on his tip of his toes.

Thad stared at Allie and cleared his throat, "Could I have this dance, ma'am?"

"Why, certainly sir," she said in her best southern drawl, waving her hands in front of her face as if she had an invisible fan.

He bowed, she curtsied, and they grabbed each other's waists with a laugh.

As they danced to the music, he looked into her eyes and she into his. The others disappeared and the music enveloped them. She closed her eyes and leaned in toward him. This time he did not hesitate. He kissed her. Not sure of what to do but sure of what he was doing, he let his lips explore hers as they swayed back and forth to the song. Immediately he knew he was wrong earlier; *this* moment would go down as the best ever.

WATCH YOUR MOUTH

The sun was shining brightly through the window and the alarm clock kept ringing like a ticked-off fire truck. Marcus rolled over and hit the snooze button, but it kept going. He hit it again and there it was again. He threw it across the room, pulling its plug from the wall, but somehow it kept ringing. After throwing a pillow at it and calling it a few choice names, he realized it was his phone.

"Hello," Marcus said, scratching out the words..

"Good morning, sunshine," Thad said with a little too much merriment. "How's the head?"

"Feels like someone's using a jackhammer on my brain," Marcus said in obvious pain.

"You put on quite a show last night," Thad said with a slight chuckle.

"Remind me to never try to outdrink KJ ever, ever, ever again," Marcus said.

Thad got to the point. "Marcus, you wouldn't happen to know where Allie lives, would you?"

"Sure, man," Marcus said, "but I promised you I wouldn't play match-maker." Marcus was enjoying this irony as much as he could with a five-alarm hangover.

"Ha ha, very funny," Thad replied. "Don't make me come over there and blow a whistle in *your* ear."

"Ha ha ok," Marcus said, "she lives about six miles out of town. Take 50 East, turn right on 99 South, left on 130, left on P, left on 140, end of the road. It's a big white farmhouse. Don't know the number, but you can't miss it."

"Thanks, man, "Thad said.

Marcus answered, "You're welcome."

"Try two aspirin and a beer with Tabasco," Thad said. "It'll clear that hangover right up. See ya."

"Yea, talk to you later," Marcus said, hanging up the phone and covering his face with the one pillow left on the bed.

Thad checked his watch. 10:30 a.m. He wanted to talk to Allie. He thought about that kiss outside of Phil's Grill all night. He thought about how nice it would be to be back with her, here in his hometown. He thought about children, maybe a dog in the yard. Going to sleep next to her. Waking up next to her. Growing old with her.

But reality began to set in. He lived and worked in DC. Hell, he worked all over the world. He loved photography, but the traveling was taking its toll. Still, could he make a living as a photographer in Emporia? And what if Allie wasn't really interested in anything serious? What if she was? What if she was just rebounding? There were too many questions, and Thad didn't have the answer to any of them. He only knew he needed to talk to her, so he pointed his SUV east and headed down Highway 50.

After one right and a few lefts, he saw her house just as Marcus said. He turned down a long dirt driveway lined with redbud trees on one side and a white three-rail fence on the other. The trees had already shed their radiant pink blossoms earlier in the summer. Thad could only imagine how beautiful they must have looked in the spring. His tires crunched the rocky ground as he rolled to a stop behind Allie's Mustang. The house was two stories tall with a black shingle roof. It was brilliant white with a black door and black shutters. It had a white, four-columned front porch with rocking chairs that barely moved in the wind. He noticed a shed near the back of the house adorned in the same white and black configuration. The grass was a deep green and well manicured. The home could have been a postcard for midwestern American farmhouses.

Thad put it in park and made his way to the front door. He could see the Cottonwood River gently rolling its waters along its banks as it curled around the end of Allie's property. He stepped onto the porch. His boots sounded like an old western movie as he walked across the wooden planks. He took a breath and exhaled. Four knocks on the door left him just enough time to reconsider. Before he could change his mind, Allie was standing in the doorway. Her blond hair was pulled back in a ponytail. She was barefoot in her jeans with an old loose T-shirt marked with spots of red paint. She had a splotch of red on her cheek as well. Thad smiled at how cute she was. *How does she look so damn good without even trying?* he thought.

"Thad!" she said, surprised to see him. "I thought I was supposed to call you later on today."

"You were," he answered, "but I really wanted to come say hi. Marcus told me where you live. I hope it's ok."

"Of course. Come in," she said gesturing him into the house. "I'm sorry I'm such a mess."

Thad thought she must have been joking.

"I was in the middle of painting my cabinets. I've been working on fixing this place up since Danny and I…well, you know." She forced an embarrassed smile.

"Hey, you look great. Are you kidding?" he said. "Red is so your color."

He pointed to the red paint on her cheek. She looked in a large mirror hung in the foyer near the door and feverishly wiped the color to no avail.

"I cannot paint without getting more on me than what I'm supposed to be painting," she said, still wiping.

Thad entered the old home and instantly noticed her imprint on the place. The way things were arranged. The impeccable and elegant taste. The large paintings hanging on the walls. A sitting area with a small couch near the foyer for talking to guests without fully inviting them in, great for those surprise visits from Jehovah's Witnesses or politicians running for local office. Antique furniture carefully adorning the rooms. Hardwood floors that were well cared for. Large windows allowing ample sunlight in and beautiful vistas out. Everything about it was Allie.

"Your home is beautiful," he said as they made their way toward the dining room.

"Thank you," she said. "But it's a mess. One day I'm gonna have it the way I like it." She grabbed a magazine that lay haphazardly on the dining room table and placed it on a nearby buffet table.

"So to what do I owe the honor?" she asked as they sat down on her living room couch. Thad was glad he made it past the small one in the sitting area.

"Umm, Allie," Thad said, "I've been thinking a lot lately." He was trying to choose his next words carefully. "I know I've been gone a long time. I am constantly on the road. And I know you have your life here."

"Yes?" she said, looking at him intensely.

"I know you just got out of a relationship," he said, "and I don't want to be tromping in here all 'Hey, I'm back' and 'hey, let's hang out' and 'hey, you seeing anybody?' You know?"

"What?" she said, totally confused.

Obviously he didn't choose his words that carefully after all. He tried again. "Well, see, I've been thinking that maybe I should—"

He could not finish the sentence. The front door swung open hard. It banged into the wall, causing the foyer mirror to tilt from the force. Allie and Thad both snapped their heads toward the noise.

"What the...?" Allie said, rising from the couch.

Thad rose with her. He barely made a step toward the front door when he heard him.

"Who the hell is parked in my driveway?" Danny screamed.

"Danny, what the hell are you doing here?" Allie yelled back as she and Thad hurried into the sitting area.

Danny was obviously drunk or high or both.

"It's my damn house, bitch," he said with his eyes trained on Thad.

"Watch your mouth," Thad said, keeping his eyes trained on Danny.

"Who the hell are you, pretty boy?" Danny said taking one step closer.

"Danny, just leave," Allie said, standing between the two men.

He ignored her and took another small step closer to Thad. "You screwing my wife?" he said.

"Danny, *go home*," Allie ordered. "I'm not your wife. This is not your house!"

Danny stalked to the right, never losing eye contact with Thad. "You think you can come in here, screw her, and take my place?

"If you open that cesspool of a mouth one more time, I'm gonna rip your tongue out of your throat," Thad warned.

Allie turned to Thad. "Thad, stop," she said.

"Thad…Thad Taylor? Old lover boy back in town, hey?" Danny said. "You gonna screw my wife under my roof and threaten me, lover boy?" Spittle flew from his mouth with every word.

"Danny, if you don't leave, I'm calling the sheriff," Allie said.

He pushed her aside. She stumbled back, falling to the floor. Thad tried to catch her, but he was too late. She hit the floor, landing on her side. Danny took advantage of Thad's chivalry and delivered a right hook to his cheek. Caught off guard, Thad stumbled back but did not lose his footing. He turned to see Danny's fist lunging toward his face. He slid his head to the left just enough, causing Danny to miss his target and go flailing in the direction of his swing. Thad rolled around and caught him with an elbow to the back of his head. Danny continued on his path toward the wall, and his face planted hard into the sheetrock, leaving an indentation of his forehead. Thad grabbed him from behind and placed him in a chokehold, pressing Danny's head forward with his left hand while squeezing his neck backward with his right arm. Danny was doing his best to scratch and pull at

Thad's head, but Thad had him, and there was nothing Danny could do. He could feel the lightheadedness setting in as Thad dragged him backward. He clawed at Thad's arms as his feet kicked helplessly across the hardwood floor.

"Stop it," Thad heard Allie say from behind him, "you're killing him." But he did not release his grip. He learned a few things in some difficult situations, in some very bad places over the years. On one assignment, NGM had embedded him with a Special Forces group in Afghanistan, and they taught him a trick or two about hand-to-hand combat. The one thing they made sure he understood: never let your opponent have another shot at you once you had the upper hand. So he strengthened his grip even tighter. He could hear Danny gurgle.

"Stop it, Thad, please," she screamed. Tears were beginning to form in her eyes. "Thad!" She slapped him hard across his face.

The sting pulled Thad back into reason. He released his stranglehold, and Danny fell to the floor. He was sucking in long gasps of air and holding his throat. He coughed in between breaths. Thad breathed hard and his eyes filled with readiness as he kept his gaze fixed on his enemy. Allie knelt down beside Danny and tried to help him as best she could. Once he started breathing normally, she helped him up and walked him to the door. He was stumbling, more from intoxication than the beating he just took. He looked down at the floor as he passed Thad. Thad just stood there, watching Allie help him out of the house. Danny started crying like a child, apologizing and saying how much he missed her. She sat him down in a rocking chair as he sobbed uncontrollably. Thad watched through the window as she took out her cell phone. She dialed Danny's brother and asked him to come get him.

"Can you bring someone to drive his truck back home?" she asked. He was in no shape to do it himself.

She stayed in the rocking chair next to Danny as they waited for his brother to arrive. Thad could not hear what they were talking about, but Danny had calmed down considerably. He saw Allie place her hand on Danny's arm, and he felt the fires of jealousy rise up inside. He watched as Danny's brother hugged Allie and took Danny to his car. He saw someone else get into Danny's truck. The two cars sped away with a cloud of dust chasing them as they rolled down the long driveway.

TWO ASPIRIN, A BEER, AND TABASCO

Marcus lifted the pillow off of his head and reached for his cell phone. He peered through squinted eyes at the time on its display.

"One o'clock," he said to himself. "Ohhhh…never again," he mumbled.

Just sitting up caused a searing pain to start at his left temple and shoot directly behind his eyes.

"Owww," he groaned. He grabbed his head with both hands.

He was in his boxers. No idea how he got in bed nor how he got undressed, for that matter. He just hoped Thad had brought him in and put him to bed. The other explanation might involve finding his clothes all over town or in a parking lot at Phil's Grill or God knew where. He was relieved to see them piled in the corner.

"You're a good man, Thad," he said with a gravelly voice.

He stumbled into the kitchen. His mouth tasted like stale buttermilk and cigarettes.

"Did I smoke last night?" he thought smacking his lips together, tasting the used side of an ashtray. He hadn't lit one up since graduating high school. During Marcus's senior year of high school, he saw his dad die of throat cancer, and no way was he going through that. He would've liked to say he missed the bastard, but let's be honest, bastards are hard to miss. The last time his father hit him was the day before they diagnosed him with cancer. Marcus could not even remember what the fight was about, but he remembered he wore a sling on his arm for a week. Rosie was so mad, it took all Marcus could do to keep him from confronting his father.

"Marcus, why don't you let me smack some sense into that asshole?" Rosie asked him the night he came over for help with his arm.

Rosie knew it was a bad one if Marcus asked for help. Marcus convinced him to let it go, that he was graduating soon and would be out on his own soon anyway. "I can handle it for a few more months," he said. Truth was, Marcus loved his dad. He hated himself for it, but he did love him. He knew his father had demons to fight; sometimes the fights just spilled over to include him.

When he came home from school that day, his dad was sitting in the living room with the lights off, smoking in his recliner. Marcus was expecting the same old sobbing with an "I'm sorry, I need help" line.

But this time his father said, "Sit down, we need to talk, man-to-man."

Marcus sat on the old sofa, across the room from him. He took care not to hurt his sore arm as he eased onto the couch. He did not say a word. His dad put the cigarette to his lips and took a long, deep draw through the filter. He held it for a few seconds, tipped his head slightly backward, and slowly let the white smoke float from his mouth and nose. He tapped the ashes into an empty beer can and looked at his son.

"How's your arm?" his dad asked.

Marcus looked at the splinted wing but did not answer.

His dad pursed his lips and nodded as if he understood. "Doctor says I got cancer," he spoke through the rising smoke.

Marcus blinked but said nothing.

"I got six months, seven maybe," he said.

Marcus still didn't speak.

His dad took another drag on the cigarette. "When I'm gone, all this will be yours," he said, laughing, followed by a deep, visceral cough.

Marcus had noticed his father coughing a lot recently. He just figured it was smoker's cough. How right he was—it was the worst kind of smoker's cough. Marcus stood up and walked toward his room. He stopped at his dad's chair and stared down at the man he feared so much. He put his good hand on his dad's shoulder and almost spoke, but no words came. He turned and headed to his room, leaving his father to contemplate his own fate.

Six months was not enough time to make up for four decades of brutality. The math just didn't add up. In the end, Marcus and his uncle Mike were the only two at his father's bedside when he died. They would have been the only two at his funeral if Thad, Rosie, Allie, and KJ hadn't shown up.

After his dad passed away, his uncle Mike helped him get on his feet. He turned eighteen a month to the day after his father's death. Uncle Mike helped him get a loan for his first home, gave him a secondhand car to drive around, and taught him the pawn shop business. Thank God for Uncle Mike.

"Beer, aspirin, and Tabasco," Marcus said to his dog, Scrappy, who wandered into the kitchen upon hearing his master's voice. "What the hell, Scraps, I can't feel any worse. If I'm lucky it will kill me. You have my permission to chew on my bones if I am so inclined to perish."

He poured a can of beer into a glass and added enough Tabasco to turn it slightly red. He popped the top off a bottle of aspirin, which is quite a feat when you're hung over. He threw two pills to the back of his throat and washed them down with the Tabasco beer.

"God, that's awful." He choked the words out.

He turned up the glass and finished the elixir, hoping for its magic to work soon. He flopped down onto the couch, waiting for either the comfort of modern medication or the sweet release of death, whichever came first. Scrappy jumped up beside him and laid his head in his master's lap. Marcus rubbed his buddy's ears and closed his eyes.

He came to with a knocking at the front door. Checking his watch, he figured he slept for about an hour on the couch. His head felt significantly better. *Thad knows what he's talking about,* he thought to himself.

He headed to the door at the second knock. "I'm coming," he said, "hold your horses."

He opened the door to find Kate standing on his steps. She was dressed in a long-sleeved white blouse and navy blue skirt with heels. Her dark hair was straight and silky.

"KJ!" he said, surprised. "I didn't know you were coming over. Then again, I don't know a lot about what we said last night." He rubbed his forehead.

"If I would have known we were dressing down," she said, "I would have shown up in my underwear."

Marcus realized he was in his boxers and felt more than embarrassed, but at that point he was committed. He invited her in and quickly excused himself to dress more appropriately.

While he slid into his old blue jeans and a T-shirt, the thought of Kate in her underwear crossed his mind. He ran to the bathroom and ran a comb through his hair and a brush through his teeth. After a quick rinse of mouthwash, he looked in the mirror.

"Best we can do on short notice," he said to his mirror image.

He stepped back into the living room to find Kate playing with Scrappy.

"Scraps, leave her alone," he said.

"He's fine," Kate said rubbing his head, "he's a cutie pie. Yes, he is." She spoke to the dog like she was talking to a baby.

"KJ, you wanna drink?" Marcus offered.

"After last night, I don't want a drink for a long time," she said through a small laugh.

"I hear ya," Marcus said, "me, too." He sat down beside her. "Did I smoke last night?"

She grinned at him. "We both did," she said.

"Man," he said, "you're a bad influence."

He smiled at her to make sure she knew he was only joking. She winked back to let him know he might be right.

"I hope I did not do anything to embarrass myself, or you, last night," he said, scratching his head. "It's all kinda fuzzy."

"Well, if you don't count your dance moves, then we're all good," she said, laughing.

He laughed along with her. Looking at her outfit, he said, "Now I see why they call you 'Doctor.' You look great…but that doesn't mean you didn't look great last night, too."

She smiled at him at and looked closely at the man in front of her. Although she hadn't been home very much over the years, she had kept up with him. They e-mailed, called, did the social media thing, even video chatted. She had known him for years. She had been through some crazy times with him, both good and bad. There had always been a special bond between them. She loved all of her friends, Thad, Rosie, and Allie, but with Marcus it was different. She spent more than one night losing sleep worrying about him living with his father. She was both proud of and impressed with the man he had become, despite everything he went through. He was still that funny, silly little boy, but he was also a strong, hard-working, dependable man. She looked closely, and she liked what she saw. She had always liked what she saw.

"Marcus," she said, "sorry I dropped by unannounced, but I wanted to talk to you alone."

"Sure, KJ," he said.

"I'm leaving tonight," she said, "heading back to work. Those whales won't wait." She smiled. "The thing is, when Rosie died, it got me thinking about what's really important." She put her hands on his. "And you're really important to me."

"You're important to me, too." He smiled back at her.

"Let's make each other a promise," she said seriously, "to always stay in touch, to always make an effort to see each other…always, Marcus… always."

He looked into her eyes and felt what he knew was in his heart all this time: true love. "Always," he said.

This was his longtime friend, one of his closest. He couldn't lie; he had thought about her romantically more than once. She was a beautiful woman. She was smart, successful, and cared more for him than just about anyone in his life. But this was Kate, Katey Jo…this was KJ. He wanted to kiss her so bad he ached. He thought she was feeling what he was feeling, but if he was wrong, then their friendship could be forever altered. She lived in Alaska; he was still in Emporia. She was a scientist; he owned a pawn shop. She was brilliant; he was, well, he was Marcus. But in the end, life is about chances you take and opportunities you miss. This was one opportunity he was not going to miss.

He stared into her eyes and she into his. He leaned in to kiss her, and she met him more than halfway. They kissed a long, slow passionate kiss. It felt like nothing Marcus had ever experienced in his life. Even when he married his ex-wife, there was never this complete, utter feeling of love. He did not want to let her go, but she slowly let her lips leave his. She put both of her hands on his face and smiled. She let him go and stood up to leave.

"I've got to go," she said still smiling. "I love you."

He followed her to the door and out to her rental car. She let the window down as she started the engine. Marcus had his hands on the roof of the car, leaning in to make sure Kate heard him.

"Always, Kate…always," he kissed her one more time, backed away from the car, and watched her drive away. It is a special love when best friends find it together. Scrappy stood beside him and barked.

"I know," Marcus said to his faithful companion, "don't worry, we will see her again soon."

He rubbed Scrappy's ears and they headed back inside. Today was the best day in Marcus Pawley's life.

VAGABOND FOR DINNER, ANYONE?

Rosie sat by the fire watching his friends slow-dance to the music pouring out of Marcus's radio. Bored, he started rummaging through their provisions. Coming across a can of pudding, he popped the top and dipped in a finger to taste the creamy dessert.

"Not tapioca," he said, to his own delight, and began devouring the treat. Just then, he thought he saw something move in the bushes. He stopped eating and looked hard in that direction. He squinted and focused, but this time he saw nothing. Satisfied, he turned his attention back to the pudding.

Rosie was humming along with Frankie Valli's smooth tenor voice, when he briefly saw the movement again. This time he froze. It's spooky enough in the woods at night, let alone with things moving in them. *Old Man Booker?* Rosie wondered in disbelief. With one finger still in the can of chocolate pudding, Rosie slowly stood. Keeping his eye trained on the spot where he saw the movement, he slowly crept toward the bushes. He didn't say anything to his friends, partly because he didn't want to scare them, but mostly because he didn't want to sound like a big chicken. It was probably nothing—a squirrel, a deer, maybe just his imagination.

About five feet from the bushes, he came to a stop. Peering through the darkness into the thick brush, he saw nothing. Convincing himself he had imagined it and not really wanting to trek into the bushes anyway, he began to turn back to the group. Suddenly a large figure sprang from the darkness. He knocked Rosie down and dashed toward the campfire, pushing Allie to the ground. Before anyone knew what was happening, the man was standing over Allie with a knife and screaming.

"Nobody move!" the deranged man yelled.

Nobody did move, not because they were ordered not to, but because nobody knew what was happening. A stranger had just rushed into their campsite and held a hunting knife big enough to butcher a hog. Everyone needed a moment to grasp the reality of the situation. When he grabbed Allie by her hair and jerked her up, reality set in. Allie screamed and grabbed the top of her head to try and relieve the pain. It did not help.

Thad felt anger rush through him and jumped at the man. "Let her go!" he screamed.

The large man elbowed Thad in the face, knocking him to the ground. Thad rolled in pain but only briefly. He quickly sat up, his hand pressed to the eye that had taken the brunt of the man's wrath. The others moved toward the stranger, but he placed the knife to Allie's neck.

"Everybody freeze or I'll slice her damn neck open," the man warned.

The man was wearing raggedy old clothes. His hair hadn't seen a comb in days or maybe even weeks. He smelled of booze and urine. Thad summed him up as a bum, probably a drunkard and probably in trouble with the law—after tonight, definitely in trouble with the law.

All the while, Frankie Valli and the the radio were still doing their job.

"That hurts," Allie cried.

"Shut up," the man said. "Looks like I got myself a bunch of rug rats. What the hell is a bunch of shit-kicking rug rats doing out here in these woods at night anyway?"

No one said anything except the DJ. "This one goes out to all you troublemakers out there." Frankie faded away and the unmistakable sounds of Creedence Clearwater Revival playing "Bad Moon Rising" eerily filled the night.

"Hmm, here's what I think," the man continued. "I think you guys snuck out of the house. Your mommy and daddy don't even know you're here. *Do they?*" He yelled, causing the kids to flinch and Allie to scream.

"You hurt her and I'll—" Thad warned.

"You'll what?" The man laughed. He locked his gaze on Thad. "Well, well, what do we have here? A hero. Are you a hero, boy?" He placed the knife closer to Allie's neck.

John Fogerty sang out as the lyrics foreshadowed the unfolding events.

Thad froze, mad as hell that he couldn't do anything to help Allie. He knew if he could ever get his hands on the man, he didn't care how big he was, he would beat him to a pulp. But he couldn't move. The stranger held all the cards.

"Y'all having a little *looove* party?" the man asked. "Any…hanky-panky going on?" He thrust his hips back and forth. He looked at Allie and smiled a smile that disgusted her. "Ok. Here's what we are gonna do. We are gonna go through all the shit you got in them bags over there and you are gonna give me everything I want. You got it?"

The kids nodded, and Allie stood motionless. The man directed Katey Jo to bring him the bags and lay them at his feet. She did as she was told.

"Hey, big boy," the man said to Rosie, who was still near the bushes, "bring your ass over here with the others so I can watch you. The rest of you stand right here in front of me. Don't nobody do nothing stupid like run. We out deep in the woods and it's late. You won't make it very far before I run you down and gut you like a fish."

The kids did as he ordered, slowly walking to a spot where he pointed. He still held on to Allie, but at least he let her hair go. Now he just had her by the arm but with the knife still close to her neck.

"I'm hungry," the man barked. "What do you kiddies have in there to eat? I'm talking to *you*, shithead!" He was staring right at Marcus.

Marcus jumped back a little when the man yelled at him. Startled, he said, "Uh, we have, uh, marshmallows and pudding."

"What else?" he barked. He waited while Marcus tried to get the words out. "Well, get down there and look, idiot."

Marcus fell to his knees in front of the provisions, "Umm, grape Nehis, some chips, peanut butter crackers, bologna sandwiches—"

"Bologna?" the man asked. "Give me one of them sandwiches and a grape drink."

Marcus did as instructed. He handed the man a sandwich. Reaching back in the bag, he grabbed hold of the neck of one of the drink bottles. He tightened his grip.

John Fogerty warned them a bad moon was bound to take their life. The Cottonwood rushed by, almost echoing the song.

"You wanna hit me with that there glass bottle, don'tcha, runt?" The man said, spitting pieces of bologna while he talked. "Go ahead. See if you can get to me 'fore I gut her…and you." He now held the knife at Allie's ribs.

Marcus thought better of it and slowly handed him the bottle. He remained seated by the bag while the man ate. Nobody said a word, they just all watched in disgust as he devoured the sandwich like a rabid wolf. He turned up the bottle and drank the entire soda, several large gulps at a time. The kids could see his Adam's apple ride up and down his throat as he consumed the drink.

"Ya'll got any smokes?" the man asked, looking at the kids. When no one answered, he said, "Shit, that's what I get for robbing a bunch of rug rats."

Wiping his mouth with his shirt, the stranger ordered Marcus to put everything he could into one bag. "Give me all your lunch money," the man said, bursting out a vulgar laugh, "I haven't said that in years." He continued laughing.

Except for Marcus doing the job he was ordered to do, and for Allie wiggling in the man's grip, the other kids just stood there motionless. "I ain't kiddin', you little bastards," he shouted, "give me all your money. All your allowance money, everything in your pockets." The kids did as he said and began emptying the little bit of cash they had in their pockets. Thad pulled out Abigail's necklace but quickly put that back in his pocket.

"Hey, what you got there?" the man asked Thad, spying the shiny object.

"Nothing," Thad answered.

"Don't lie to me, boy, or I'll make your other eye look as bad as that one," he warned, pointing with the knife at Thad's elbowed eye. It was already swelling and turning blue. Thad relented and pulled the necklace out of his pocket. The man grabbed it and held it up to the fire light to get a good look at it.

"Well, now, this looks like it might be old enough to be worth something," the man said with the confidence of a thief.

"It's not worth anything. We had it checked out—" Rosie began to explain.

"*I don't remember asking you a damn thing!*" the man shouted at Rosie.

Rosie froze.

While the man was focusing his attention and yelling at Rosie, Marcus slipped his hand back into his pocket. He clutched his Swiss Army knife. He quietly flipped the tiny blade open with his finger. He waited...

NO SUPERHERO

Standing on the porch with Allie, Thad was stunned by what just occurred. One minute he was talking to her about a future and the next he was nearly strangling a man to death who attacked her, only to watch her help and console that same guy. Thad had to rethink things, to step back and make sure he wasn't just caught up in a passionate moment. Maybe he was moving too fast. Yes, he was definitely moving too fast. Standing there with Allie, he watched the two cars turn onto the road.

"I'm sorry, Thad," she said, looking down.

"I wasn't going to kill him, Allie," he said. "I was going to throw his ass out."

She didn't say anything.

"Why did you help him like that?" he asked. "He just barged in here, called you names, took a swing at me…hell, he hit me!"

"I know, Thad. It's not that simple," she said.

"Seems simple to me," he said, obviously upset. "You let this asshole break into your house, call you names, push you down, hit me, and then you yell at me and even slap me while I'm defending you. Seems like you still love him." His voice rose in volume along with his anger.

"That's not true," she said.

"Then what is it?"

"It's…it's…" she stammered. "Thaddeus, you don't understand."

"Obviously, so why don't you enlighten me?" he said.

"He was my husband, Thad," she said. "I know him better than anyone. He has problems that go way beyond our divorce."

"But he's not your husband anymore," Thad protested.

"I know that," she said. "He needs help."

"Are you telling me you are going to help that SOB? 'Cause if you are, then…" He stopped.

"Then what?" she asked, her voice showing signs of anger. "Then what? Then you're gonna take your business somewhere else? What, Thad? You think you and I are back together?"

"No, I didn't say that," he said.

"No, you didn't, did you?" Allie took a step closer. "You think you can stay away from here for years at a time and come swooping back in like some kind of superhero or something? Like I can't do anything without you. Like I can't even love again without you."

Thad didn't answer. He just let his anger build.

"I have a life, you know," she continued. "I'm not some helpless little girl."

"Allie, I just saw you ex-husband storm into *your* house and *punch me*, and you're mad at *me*?! What the hell? He is your *ex*!"

"You can't just be with someone for years and then all of a sudden let them completely *go!*" she yelled, tears building, but more from anger than anything else. She was beyond upset at having to defend herself.

"You mean like you did to me?" He knew it when he said it. That one cut deep.

"Asshole." She started crying as she ran back into the house.

Thad stood there on the porch, looking at the rocking chair sway back and forth from where Allie brushed it.

"What in the hell just happened?" he said to himself.

He wanted to go back inside, but he didn't know what to say. The love of his life was inside crying, and if he went back in there, he would probably just make things worse. Besides, he was still pretty damn mad himself. How could she slap him like that? In front of her ex-husband?

He decided it would be best if he simply left. Maybe they would both calm down later and talk about it. Maybe she would never talk to him again. He reached in his pocket for his keys and headed back to his Navigator. He turned the key and the quiet engine barely hummed. Satellite radio broke the silence as the Bee Gees sang "Too Much Heaven." Thad stared at the radio for a moment.

Listening to the words of the song he said, "That's the damn truth. Nobody gets too much heaven around here."

He put the car into reverse, backed around and eased it into drive. He looked in his review mirror as he drove slowly down the driveway. Waiting, almost hoping, that Allie would appear in the doorway and run after him. But no Allie and no one running. He turned onto the road and made his way back to town. He picked up his phone, but no text from her, either. No sooner did he place the phone back into the cup holder, than it rang. He didn't even look to see who it was. He knew.

"Allie, I'm sorry," he said into the phone.

"Sorry for what?" Marge from *National Geographic* asked.

"Marge?" Thad asked, surprised.

"Yes, honey, it's only Marge," she answered.

"I'm…I'm sorry," he said, caught off guard. "Yeah, Marge, what's up?"

"I hope I'm not disturbing the funeral or anything," Marge answered.

"No, it's ok," he replied. "So what's up?"

She delivered the bad news. "Ken wanted me to tell you we need those shots from Syria sooner than expected, He said by tomorrow night."

"Tomorrow night!" Thad was not happy. *This day just keeps getting worse,* he thought. In an upset voice he said, "I've been here only two days, just buried my best friend, and he wants these edits four days early?"

"I know, I know," she said. "Don't kill the messenger."

"I'm not mad at you, Marge," Thad said. "Sometimes I think they want the impossible."

"You're right," she said, "they want the impossible, but you're the one who makes the impossible possible." She was giving her best pep talk.

Thad sighed and looked out the window of his SUV, watching the green grass flow by like an emerald ocean. "Ok," he said, "tell Ken…

tell Ken that I will get him what I can, but he's just going to have to wait for the rest." He hung the phone up without saying goodbye.

Thad was frustrated. Most people do not realize the art and work that go into a published picture. A picture that seems so routine, so casual or so energized. Rarely does an image just appear on camera and become the photograph that a viewer sees. Hardly, it takes hours of editing each image. The light needs to be just right. The shadows need to provide dramatic effect. The color, the hue, the intensity, so many factors that need to be perfected to show off the quality of the image and relay the story that the photographer is trying to tell. And Thad had over forty such images.

"It never ends," he said to himself.

He wondered how he was going to get this all done in time. Ken wanted four days of work done in two, and then there was Allie. He couldn't let this hang in the air with her. He couldn't think straight. He needed someone to talk to. Marcus was as close to a brother as Thad had, but some things were just not up his alley. Relationship advice...about Allie...definitely not his strong suit. Thad needed to clear his head. He had made it back to town and headed toward his mom's house. He decided to take a left onto Constitution Street and make his way to Peter Pan Park. He parked his car and walked into the old park. *The place looks better*, he thought as he strolled through the beautiful green grass and old trees. He stopped by the bronze statue of Peter Pan and noticed it seemed to be cleaner than last time he was here.

The park got its unusual name from a dedication made years ago. William Allen White dedicated the land to the city in the 1920s in memory of his daughter, Mary, who died from a riding accident at the young age of seventeen. "She was a Peter Pan who refused to grow up," Mr. White said of his daughter. Therefore the park was named as such. Beauty born of tragedy.

Thad took a seat on a bench by the children's wading pool. There was no child there today to splash the cool water, so Thad decided to take it upon himself to test the pool. He took off his socks and shoes and rolled up his pants legs. One foot in, then the other, and he smiled at the sight of himself. He moved the clear water in ripples as he paced in circles around the pool. He thought of all the times he would come to the park with Rosie and Marcus. He thought of the night of their adventure, with Allie and Katey Jo coming along. He kicked the water up, splashing the edge of the pool. Sometimes a big kid needed to feel like a little kid. He was feeling better, lost in the time-traveling effects of the wading pool, when he heard a child's voice.

"You're too big for the pool," said a little girl standing next to the wading pool. "It's for kids, not grown-ups."

Thad was surprised at the little girl's admonishment.

"Don't you think it's big enough to share?" he asked the child with a friendly smile.

"Mama said it's for little kids," the child said. "Don't you have grown-up stuff to do?"

Thad thought about that question. Indeed he did have "grown-up stuff to do." He needed to figure out what to do with his job. He needed to figure out what to do with Allie. He needed to figure out how to figure that out. The child's mother walked up behind the little girl and apologized for her bluntness.

Stepping out of the pool, Thad smiled at the woman. "It's ok, ma'am," he said. "Sometimes kids hit the nail on the head."

He slipped on his socks and shoes and walked back to the car. Leaning against the driver side door, he pulled out his cell phone and dialed

Kate. It rang five times and then went to voicemail. He waited for the ridiculously long instructions on how to leave a simple message and began doing so after the beep. Before he could get the first word out, he was interrupted by an incoming call. He pulled the phone away from his ear and saw that Kate was promptly returning his call.

"Hi, Kate," he said.

"Hey, Thaddeus," she returned the greeting. "Sorry, I was just getting through security at the airport. What's up?"

"Nothing," he said, "I just wanted to ask your advice."

"Shoot," she said.

"Well, it's about Allie…and myself," he said.

"Ohhhh, juicy. Ok, what do you want to know?" she asked.

"You know how I feel about Allie, right?" Thad asked.

"Thad," she said, "everyone knows how you feel about Allie."

"Ok, ok," he said, "we had a big fight today. Her ex shows up while I'm at her house—"

Kate interrupted. "And you guys were doing it!"

"No, Kate," he said a little perturbed, "we weren't doing it." He paused. "I was going there to talk to her about, you know, maybe seeing how things might go, you know, together." He was getting flustered and embarrassed. "But her ex busted in and started pushing her and swinging at me, and I had to put him down."

"You shot him?" Kate asked surprised.

"No, I didn't shoot him," Thad said, frustrated. "I meant 'put him down' as in 'put the guy in a headlock and throw him out.'"

"Oh," Kate said.

"Anyway," he continued, "Allie yelled at me and slapped me when I grabbed the guy, and I guess it rubbed me the wrong way. I felt like I was there defending her and myself from this drunk asshole, and I got yelled at. Meanwhile, she sits with him and put her hands on his arm until his brother shows up to drive him home. I love her, Kate. I went there to tell her that, to see if maybe there was something there we could explore. Now I don't know if she still loves her ex-husband, if he will always come between us, if…hell, I don't know. I guess I just wanted to find out what you thought."

"Thad," Kate said, "all I know is, when you two are together, there is so much electricity in the air, somebody could get shocked just standing near the both of you. Allie will always have some feelings deep down for Danny, but that doesn't mean she is in love with him. The bottom line is this: is there any way you can see your future without her in it?"

She was right. Thad knew the answer to that question. No.

"You're pretty smart…for a fish doctor," Thad said.

"And you're pretty dumb if you don't go work it out with her," Kate said. "Take care of yourself, Thad."

"You too, Kate." Thad hung up the phone and looked at his watch. The day was slipping away quickly. He thought about calling Allie, but there was something he needed to take care of first. One thing was for sure, he knew exactly what he wanted…Allie. He took in the day's events and shook his head at getting in a fight at his age. Still, sometimes a man had to do what a man had to do. It made him think of a fight years ago. One that nearly cost him his life.

JUST ANOTHER DEMON

This wasn't the first time Marcus stared a demon in the face. He had already fought off one earlier in the night. *What was one more?* he thought. He rotated his hidden pocketknife so the blade was in prime striking position.

The stranger was looking at the necklace he had just snatched from Thad's hand.

He fumbled with the latch until it popped open and then read the inscription out loud, "*To Abigail. Love, Mom and Dad.* Who the hell is Abigail?"

No one answered.

He snapped the locket closed and commanded Marcus to give him another grape drink. Doing as he was told, Marcus grabbed the last bottle left in the bag and handed it to him. He was sitting right there, right next to the man. If he could get the small knife out of his pocket without being noticed, maybe he would have a chance to stab the son of a bitch in the leg. That just might buy them enough time to escape.

The stranger finished off the soda and let out a large burp. He was obviously not at all concerned about his prisoners. He still had Allie by the arm, but he had let his knife slide away from her a little. Marcus slowly lifted his Swiss Army knife out of his pocket, keeping his eyes on the vulgar man. He managed to do so unnoticed, at least by the stranger. Thad saw him slide the weapon out of his pocket. They made eye contact with each other. Thad shook his head "no" in a barely noticeable motion. Marcus shook his "yes" with the same degree of motion. Cupped in one hand, he was positioning the blade when the stranger spoke up.

"Hey, what are you two idiots shaking your heads about?" he asked Marcus and Thad. "You planning some tough-guy stuff with Mr. Hero over here?" he said directly to Marcus. Marcus froze. "Yeah, you want to get me, don't ya? How 'bout you, big boy?" he said, turning his eyes to Rosie. "Well, just maybe I want to get you." He pointed the knife at Rosie.

Marcus held his pocketknife so tight in his hand, he was beginning to get a prickly sensation in his fingers. He had to make sure the man did not see it or it would be over, maybe over for good. He could feel his stomach turn with nervousness.

Allie tried to pull away, so the stranger tightened his grip on her arm.

"Where you going, sweetheart?" he asked through his stained teeth.

Allie didn't say anything. She just gave him an "eat shit and die" look. She refused to cry; she was as tough as she was beautiful.

"Oh no, I'm not lettin' you go anywhere," he said with an evil grin.

Katey Jo couldn't take it anymore. "You know," she said, "you can't get us all. At least one of us will make it out of here before you can stop us. We know what you look like...and smell like." She wrinkled her nose. "Best you take what you want and get out of here before things get sequentially worse."

"Sequentially worse?" The stranger laughed. "Who the hell do we got here? Little Miss Smarty Panties."

His smile disappeared and his eyes grew evil. "Maybe I don't need to gut all of you. Maybe I'm just gonna gut you, 'cause believe me, pretty little bookworm, I will catch you first." He snarled at her.

Marcus looked at Katey Jo with eyes that begged her not to push the stranger.

The stranger quickly changed his attitude. He let out a small chuckle and said, "Now, kiddies, we all know that I can take what I want and do what I want here. You know why we know that? Because I am bigger than you." He began to show anger again as he raised his voice. He continued, "And Mr. Knife here is so big, he can go clean through your chest and pierce your pathetic spine like it's a damned toothpick."

Mr. Fogerty kept singing warning them all of taking an eye for an eye. Satisfied he had gotten the kids' attention, he squeezed Allie's arm and redirected his gaze toward her. "You are a pretty thing, ain't ya?" he said, "How old are you, fifteen, sixteen?"

Allie did not answer. He shook her and yelled, "How old are you, damn it?"

"Fourteen, I'm fourteen," she said.

"Fourteen?" he said, surprised. "You're a young one. Tell me young one, you ever been with a man?"

Rosie clenched his fist in anger but was helpless to do anything. Allie looked away, toward Thad. She was tough, but she was scared. They all knew where this was headed.

The stranger smelled Allie's hair. "Damn, you smell good," he said. He played with her hair, running the long blade through it. "Naw, I bet you ain't never been with a man." He smelled her hair again and said, "Well, since I'm taking what I want, I'm taking a shining on taking you."

He stuck his rough, brown-stained tongue out and slid it up Allie's neck. She slapped him across his face. It did not faze him.

"A fighter," he said, "I like 'em rough." He slowly slid the big knife down Allie's shirt, stopping on her breast, moving the blade in a circular motion around her nipple.

"Please," Allie begged. She didn't want to, but she could not stop the pleading. Tears started forming in her eyes, thinking about what this vulgar human being was about to do to her.

"You're a pig!" Katey Jo shouted.

The stranger just smiled at back at Katey Jo while he let his knife fondle Allie's breast. The evil grin he gave her meant she would be next.

Thad was turning red. He looked at Rosie, and they both knew they had to act fast. The stranger was definitely preoccupied with Allie, so Thad carefully pointed his head toward Marcus in an attempt to tell Rosie about the pocketknife. Rosie looked at Marcus, and Marcus gave him a peek at the weapon. Rosie nodded. Thad nodded. Marcus nodded. Marcus held the blade with his thumb, still hiding the knife in his hand.

"Damn, girl," the man said to Allie, "you sure you're only fourteen? You've got the biggest tits I've ever seen on a fourteen-year-old girl."

Allie was squirming. Katey Jo wore an expression of fear mixed with hate. She looked at Allie as if to say, "It's ok. I'm right here." Allie looked back at Katey Jo. She was so embarrassed and ashamed...and scared.

The man popped one of Allie's buttons loose with the knife. "What do ya say, boys?" he asked, laughing. "Wanna see some titties?" He popped another one loose, exposing the top of Allie's bra.

That was it. Thad could not take it anymore. Yes, the man was bigger and had a blade large enough to slice right through him, but this was going from a robbery to a rape and probably murder. His mind raced. Adrenaline coursed though his veins, revving his heart into overdrive. Sweat was beginning to form on his forehead, even though it was a cool sixty degrees. His pupils dilated and fixed on his target. His skin tingled. He was in full attack mode, like a wild animal closing in on its kill. The offensive laughter of the stranger disappeared into the background. The song on the radio sounded distorted, as if CCR was playing in a long tube. He could hear his own breathing, hear the rush of the Cottonwood River, feel the pounding of his heart in his chest. He could smell the crispness in the air and feel the slightest of breezes. His brain had taken over and turned his body into a fighting machine. The most primal of all things human.

Rosie and Marcus were breathing heavy. Steam beginning to form with each exhale. They watched, waiting for a chance. Both boys were primed and ready to move. Thad and Rosie looked at Marcus. Neither said a word, but Marcus clearly understood what they wanted.

Allie squirmed and the man still laughed and talked, but to Thad the sound moved off into the distance, and Allie faded away. He could see only the man, in slow motion, his mouth moving as he spoke, his disgusting brown teeth. Thad gave a full nod to Marcus and the boys began their attack.

Marcus raised his hand up and slammed the pocket knife deep into the stranger's foot as hard as he could. The small thin blade easily pierced the canvas shoe like paper. He could feel the metal slide off of bone and stab into the sole of the shoe. It felt like stabbing through a firm orange into a cutting board. At the exact moment Marcus stabbed the stranger's foot, Rosie and Thad lunged toward him.

The stranger howled like a wounded wolf. Before he could even bring his large knife up from Allie's breast, Rosie was tackling him up high, blocking his arms and preventing him from raising the weapon. Thad shot for the stranger's legs, hitting them with such force that he jammed one of the man's knees backward, causing a popping sound. He heard the man scream in pain once again. The stranger let Allie go as he fell backward toward the campfire, dropping his knife and Abigail's necklace. Katey Jo ran to Allie and pulled her away from the man. Thad, Rosie, and the stranger fell into the fire, sending sparks and flames in all directions. All three rolled on the ground in a deadly wrestling match. The stranger was flailing and screaming, but Thad held tight to his legs. Rosie was giving it to him for all it was worth. He relentlessly punched the man in the face. The stranger was able to kick Thad in the head; it stunned him, and he let the man go. With his free legs, the stranger kneed Rosie in the torso, but Rosie would not stop the brutality he had unleashed. The stranger finally slammed his fist into Rosie's face, which backed Rosie up enough for the man to attempt to regain his footing.

Just as the song said, a bad moon was definitely rising.

Before the stranger could steady himself, Marcus flew from out of the darkness onto his back, screaming and clawing like a wild man. The big man threw Marcus off his shoulder like a sack of potatoes. Marcus hit the ground, tumbling into his radio. When the man turned back to the other two teenagers, Thad had already pounced on him. The two of them hit the ground, rolled down the riverbank, and splashed into the rushing waters of the Cottonwood.

Thad heard Rosie scream his name as he went under the churning water. It was dark and cold.

DOWN THE RIVER THEY WENT

The force of the water surprised Thad. It was strong and persistent, applying a constant pull in every direction. It tore the stranger from his grip. He tried to kick up to the surface, but he couldn't tell if he was swimming up or swimming down. He felt something poke him in the arm. He grabbed it and immediately recognized the feeling of a tree branch. He clung tight and pulled, lifting his head just over the churning water. He caught his breath and held on with all his strength.

Water rolled down his face and splashed in his eyes and ran up his nose, burning his sinuses. He couldn't let go of the branch or he knew he would forever be lost to the waters of the Cottonwood. He blinked his eyes hard and fast, trying to clear his vision. He realized he was holding on to the branch where they found Abigail's necklace.

He looked up and saw Rosie frantically screaming and waving instructions at him. He could see his other friends rushing to the riverbank to help. He lost sight of the stranger, but he knew he wasn't clinging to the branch alongside of him.

"Climb out," Rosie screamed.

Thad was a strong swimmer. He was even planning on being a lifeguard next year. They let you at age fifteen. He could get a tan, make some money, plus he would get to watch girls in bikinis all day. As strong a swimmer as he was, he could not pull himself more than an inch or two up the branch against the rapid current. Water becomes an unstoppable force under the right conditions—and unfortunately Thad was in the right conditions.

"Climb, climb," his friends screamed.

He did not want to die, not here, not like this. He pulled and kicked with all his might and he felt himself move toward the shore.

"That's it," Marcus yelled, "a little more."

Another tug and another few inches. He was exhausted, but he was doing it. Another tug and *snap*—Thad heard the tree branch crack under the strain. Everything became fluid, the water, the branch, Thad. Everything flew away from the bank of the river. He floundered helplessly as the Cottonwood had its way with him. Down the river he went, like a child's paper boat floating on a stream. Down the river he went.

The other kids ran along the river's edge as fast as they could, following him.

"Thad!" Rosie shouted.

"Swim for the shore," one of the girls screamed. *What do you think I'm trying to do?* he thought.

He struggled to keep his head above water. He coughed and choked as water entered his throat and nostrils. *I should have told my mom and dad what we were planning tonight,* he thought. *This is going to kill them.* But he still kept kicking. He had already lost sight of his friends and was beginning to lose the sound of their voices. He thought he heard a man scream for help, but he couldn't tell if he was imagining it or if it was he doing the screaming. Down the river he went, like a leaf in a rain filled street gutter heading to the storm drain. Down the river he went.

He tilted his head back to keep the water out of his face and saw the heavens. *They are beautiful,* he thought. Time slows down, that's what everyone says; time slows down when you are dying. It sure felt that way to Thad. He began to feel like he was barely moving. He had all night to look at the stars. Floating away.

Under the river he went, like a plastic cup whose edges begin to overflow. He felt the water slide over his face, and then he was fully submerged. It was quieter, more peaceful under here. He had given up swimming, given up fighting the current. It was time, and he was at peace with that. At least he stopped that bastard from touching Allie. Hopefully they would find his body. Hopefully they would find it nearby and soon. It was getting easier now. Under the river he went.

That's when he saw her. An angel's face. Beautiful, long, flowing hair and deep piercing eyes. She floated alongside him. He cocked his head sideways and wondered who would dive in this dangerous water. He heard her speak. *Talking underwater?* he thought.

Her voice was crystal clear and surrounded him. "Thad, don't give up. Never give up...Thad...Thad..." Then she screamed so loud he grabbed his ears and kicked his feet as hard as he could.

He sprang out of the water and sucked in air like he hadn't breathed in a year. He slammed hard into something that wedged him against the relentless river current. Rocks. He had run into a large outcropping of rocks in the river. It cut his side, but the pain was quick and fleeting. He realized he was no longer washing away downstream but holding steady where he was. He continued breathing in air like it was the last he would have. He heard voices—his friends screaming his name.

He heard Rosie over them all. "Thad! Thad!"

"He's over there." Katey Jo pointed.

They ran to the river's edge and saw Thad clinging to the outcropping of stones just a few yards away.

"Thad, hang on," Allie yelled over the roaring water.

Rosie stepped into the water. The current caught him off guard and knocked his feet out from under him. He went under the water sideways, but it was shallow enough for him to catch himself. He quickly righted his position and stood tall. He dug his feet into the muddy bottom and secured himself.

"Grab my hand," he screamed to Thad.

Thad tried to let one hand go, but the current almost pulled him off of his cornerstone. He placed both hands back on the rocks.

"I can't reach you," he yelled back. "You're too far."

"Marcus, give me your belt," Rosie yelled.

Marcus had his belt off in record time, whipping it through the loops and passing it to Rosie. Rosie took another step deeper into the river. He used his strength to fight the current. Rosie removed his belt as well and interlocked the buckles, giving him a good five feet of length. He tossed it to Thad.

"Grab it," he screamed over the rushing water.

Thad tried again to grab the belt, but it was too far away. He was forced to rescind the action when he slipped a few inches with his one-handed grip. He steadied himself with both hands. He needed to focus and make the grab. Rosie threw the belt again. Thad prepared to try again. He would lunge for it on the count of three.

He counted, "One, two, thr—"

He felt something grab his arm, or someone to be more precise. The stranger was holding to the outside edge of the outcropping. He had worked his way around the corner and grabbed onto Thad, pulling himself closer to shore.

"Help me," the stranger cried.

He pulled harder, causing Thad to slip a little farther toward the edge of the rocks. Thad groaned and jerked away from him toward the shore. The man was too big. He was pulling Thad away.

"Don't let me die." The man begged.

Thad's head dipped back under the water, and he struggled to keep it up.

"If I die, you die," the stranger said, tightening his grip on Thad.

Thad kicked wildly, but the man held desperately tight, slowly pulling Thad away with him.

He grabbed the top of Thad's head with his free arm and pulled Thad under. Thad thrashed and clawed at the stranger's hand. Rosie screamed. The stranger was inching forward, slowly, slowly. He heard something over his shoulder. Looking back he saw an angel's face. She was beautiful. She smiled at him and he was captivated by her long flowing hair and piercing eyes. Time slowed down.

"Who are you?" he asked, almost calm.

The apparition floated closer and smiled. She entranced him. Almost as if she could lift him out of the water. She was right in front of him now. He could feel the kid kicking and squirming underwater. He was content to let the little bastard drown. It was his fault he was in the water anyway. And this beautiful angel was here to protect him. He could tell she would save him.

"Who are you?" he asked again.

She began to speak, "I…am…*Death!*"

Her beautiful face twisted and contorted. Her angel eyes turned to fire. Her flesh burned away, leaving bone. Her mouth opened wide, so wide that she could fit his entire head in it if she so desired. Worms crawled from her eye sockets and maggots from her nasal openings.

The stranger screamed in terror, holding both hands in front of his face in self-defense. He instantly lost his grip on Thad and the rocks. He washed away into the dark, growling waters of the Cottonwood. Down the river he went, down the river he went, the devil called his little one home, down the river he went.

RESIGNATIONS AND WILD ROSES

Thad had arrived at the floral store thirty minutes too late. It had closed at 5:00 p.m. Now he had to wait until the morning. Sitting in the parking lot, he thought long and hard about his next move. He stared at his phone, trying to decide whether to make the call or not. "Screw it," he said to the phone. He punched in the numbers to his office in DC. He waited for the familiar voice to answer. It was not her fault, but still, he let Marge know he was not happy with the rush job put on him during his best friend's funeral. He told her to let Ken know there was no way the edits would be done by the time he requested, but he would definitely have them by next week, as originally promised. After the phone conversation, Thad drove his SUV slowly through his hometown. Past the library. Past the police station. Past the high school. He missed this town, really missed it. He wondered what his life would be like in the future if he continued down the path he was on. He saw a building with a For Rent sign on the door. He thought it would make a perfect studio. He turned the vehicle onto his mother's road.

"Rose Taylor Road," he said to himself with a smile. He stopped in front of Rosie's childhood home. It was painted a weird bluish color now, and Thad didn't care for the way the current owners had let the yard go. He could see himself and Rosie and Marcus running in the grass, playing tag. Rosie stopped for a brief second and looked right into his SUV. He motioned for Thad to join them. It was so real that Thad actually waved back. Then Rosie took off chasing after the others. Thad felt a tear rolling down his cheek, and then and there he knew what he had to do.

Back at his mother's house, he spent a few hours working on the pictures to get some edits out of the way. Afterward he pulled out a piece of paper and placed it into his mother's old typewriter. No way would she have a printer in her house. He began typing.

To Ken Waller, Senior Photo Editor, NGM

Dear Ken,

I want to thank you for the wonderful opportunity you have given me at NGM. The years I have spent with the magazine have been amazing and surreal. However, I am at a point in my life that I need to reevaluate the direction in which I want to proceed. Therefore, it is with regret that I must give you my notice of resignation, effective immediately. Thank you again for the opportunity, and I wish you and the magazine nothing but the best.

Sincerely,

William Thaddeus Taylor

He folded the letter and put it in an envelope, which he planned on delivering along with the edits upon his return to Washington, DC.

The rest of the night, he had spent rehearsing what to say and what not to say to Allie, mostly what not to say. Still, no matter how he said it, it did not come out right. How do you tell a woman you're hopelessly in love with her and want to rearrange all the deck chairs on the boat to be with her? Do you dance around the bush? Do you drag out the inevitable? Do you get to the point? Thad figured the last was the best option. When dealing with matters of the heart, through to the core was usually the best bet. He fell asleep, thinking of Allie.

He was up with the sun; the smell of Mrs. Taylor's bacon frying made sure of that.

"Good morning, sleepyhead," Mrs. Taylor said to Thad as he shuffled into the kitchen. She placed two sunny-side-up eggs on his plate along with three sides of bacon and two pieces of toast.

"Sleepyhead?" Thad said scratching his head. "It's 6:00 a.m."

"Were you up late working on those pictures last night?" she asked.

Thad let out a heavy breath. "You know, Mom," he said, "do you ever wonder if you're doing what you're supposed to be doing?"

Mrs. Taylor poured him a glass of orange juice and sat down with him at the table.

"Thad," she said with all-knowing eyes, "what we are 'supposed' to be doing here on earth is whatever with whoever it is that makes us happy." She took a sip of orange juice. "Life is too short to waste on being miserable." She stroked his cheek. "Thad, my baby boy, be happy. Go get her...after you eat, of course."

"Of course," Thad said, crunching on a piece of bacon.

After a warm shower, Thad put on his best suit and headed out the door. It was 7:00 a.m. as Thad started his car. He was heading to Mary's Floral Shop, hoping he could catch Mary in the store. The sign from last night said she opened at 8:00, but Thad thought he might get lucky and get her to make an early sale. Sure enough, he pulled up to the flower shop just as Mary was unlocking the door. He had known her since high school. They had taken several classes together. Back then she was a looker, but the years had not been Mary's friend. She had overly tanned skin and a wrinkled face, making her look years older then she really was. *Too many years in the tanning bed,* Thad thought to himself.

He smiled and said, "Well, Mary Boatright, how have you been?"

Mary turned and looked at the stranger for a brief second before the light came on and she recognized who he was.

"Thaddeus Taylor, is that you?" she asked with surprise.

"Yes, ma'am, in the flesh," he said, smiling. "Came down for Rosie's funeral."

Mary frowned. "That was so sad."

"Yes, it was," he said. "You did a great job with the flowers. They were beautiful."

"Thank you very much," she said. "I know you two were close."

Thad pondered that thought for the briefest of moments and then said, "I know you don't open till eight, but I was hoping you might be able to put something together for me right now."

"Of course, Thad," she said. "What are you wanting?"

"Wild prairie rose?" he answered with a question.

"No problem," she said. "Come on in."

He offered his thanks and entered the store with her while she held the door open. Mary had a quaint floral shop. She had various flower arrangements readymade in a large glass refrigerator. There was a section just for funeral arrangements. She had an assortment of greeting cards for every emotion one might feel the need to express, with someone else's words, that is. There were knickknacks and balloons strewn throughout the shop. Of course, you could order a custom arrangement and watch Mary make it while you wait.

She returned from the back with a handful of purple wild prairie roses. They began to reminisce, as folks often do when time has paved a long road between them, and Mary worked on a nice arrangement for him.

"So are you married?" she asked.

"Uh, no, I'm not." Thad kept it quick and to the point.

Snipping some stems, she continued prying. "Whose name do you want on the card?"

"No card, thanks." Thad bunted the question.

Finally getting directly to it, Mary asked, "Let me guess. These are for Allie McNeal?"

Somewhat off-put, Thad responded, "It seems like the whole town is interested in me and Allie...and it's Thompson now." Regretting that he sounded a little harsh, he continued in a nicer tone. "I just remembered these are her favorite flowers, so I thought I'd surprise her with some. That's all."

"Thompson?" Mary said, looking up at Thad. "That's right. I remember now. She and Danny broke up. That was sad." Realizing that Thad might not think their situation was all that sad, she immediately corrected herself. "But it's good too 'cause Danny was no good for her."

She continued trimming the flowers. Thad wasn't sure what to say or if he should even say anything, so he just watched Mary place the arrangement in a vase.

Breaking the awkward silence, Mary said, "You know, Thad, I've always found that if it's meant to be, it's meant to be." The older skin she now wore made her look wiser than her years.

"That's the second time I've heard someone tell me that since I've been here," Thad said with wonder. Showing a small grin, Thad shook his head in agreement. She handed him the purple flowers with baby's breath mixed in, and he handed her his AMEX card. Mary gave him his receipt and he thanked her. On his way out the door, she spoke up one more time.

"Thad," she said, causing him to stop in the middle of the doorway and look back, "love has a way of working things out. Good luck."

She gave him a big smile. He returned the gesture and let the door close behind him.

"If it's meant to be, it's meant to be," he said, looking in the rear view mirror. He started the engine and drove away.

VOICES IN YOUR HEAD

Thad's head shot up from the water like a beach ball that was held under and let go. He made a loud noise as he sucked in one lungful of air after another. He grabbed the rocks, coughing and choking the water out of his throat.

"Thad, hold on," Rosie yelled. Hold on, he did. Although his grip was tight on the rocks, he was losing the battle. The Cottonwood River was winning. He could feel his fingertips rip as he slipped one inch at a time on the rocks. It took most of his energy just to keep his head above the black water.

Rosie tossed the coupled belt again, but it did not reach. Rosie knew he had to go into the water farther. He also knew that every small step he took could mean his death. But Paul Rose was a big boy, a big boy with a big heart and there was no way in hell he was going to stand this close to his best friend, his brother, and watch the Cottonwood take him. He took another tiny step closer to Thad. Still another step and this time the water grabbed his foot and pulled hard. Rosie went under. The mud was dangerously slick, and Rosie was slipping every time he tried to stand.

I'm going to drown, he thought as his head bobbed in and out of the water.

Panic was setting in as Rosie tried and tried to regain his footing. He was barely getting any air in between the brief moments his head appeared above the water. He could hear his friends screaming on the riverbank above him. *God help me,* Rosie thought…That's when he heard it.

"Stand up, Rosie," a soft voice said. "Stand up, Rosie," the voice said again.

The pace of the water seemed to slow down. Rosie relaxed. He didn't have time to wonder who the voice belonged to, but he knew it was too close to be his friends. They were all on the riverbank yelling. Slipping like a newborn colt, he dug the side of his foot in the muddy bottom and planted it steady. He pushed hard with his strong arms until his head was completely out of the water. He regained his balance slowly and righted himself.

He looked up to find Thad closer, close enough to reach the belt if he could just get it into his hands. He wrapped one side of the leather around his right hand and tossed the free end toward Thad. This time the belt found its target. Thad grabbed it with his left hand and pulled tight. He tried to let his right hand go, but fear had the better of him.

"Let go of the rocks," Rosie yelled.

Thad tried, but once again fear would not let him.

"I've got you," Rosie yelled over the roaring water. "Trust me."

Thad knew he had no other choice. He was exhausted and losing his grip. He knew Rosie was risking his life for him. He worried his big friend wouldn't be big enough to pull him in against the current. But it was now or never. He wrapped the leather tight around his hand. He took a deep breath and let the rocks go. His feet flew out from under him and water careened into his face, but he held tight to the leather strap. He had to breathe in between large amounts of river water and foam.

Rosie leaned back with all his might as his friend let go of the rocks. He let out a loud yell as he pulled his friend as hard as he could. Thad couldn't have weighed more than 130 pounds, but with the force of the river pulling on him, he was double that. The weight surprised Rosie, and he leaned back even more. The boys stayed in this position for twenty seconds or so, as if they were caught in a deadly battle of tug o' war.

I can't hold him. The thought began racing through Rosie's mind. The connected belts began to show signs of strain, and Rosie was worried they would not hold together.

Then the same angelic voice landed on his ear, "Pull, Rosie...pull."

He did not know where the strength came from; he only knew there was no way he was letting go of the belt. He yelled like a weightlifter going for a new max as he pulled even harder on the belt. Thad felt his body being dragged toward the shore. He was able to get a foot on the ground. He grabbed the muddy bottom with all fours and crawled toward the river's edge. He felt the mud squish between his fingers while he held on to the belt and crawled. But the mud was too soft and the river was too fast. He kept slipping back down the riverbank. Thad knew he wasn't going to be able to make it back to the shore. He was more worried about his best friend. He knew Rosie would never let go of the belt. He couldn't let his friend die with him. Allie, Katey Jo, and Marcus were all yelling for him to keep going. Rosie was trying as hard as he could. His strength impressed Thad, but it was giving out; there just wasn't enough traction.

His friends would make sure he was found. He knew they would be upset at watching him drown, but he was actually at peace with it. Thad was in the process of letting go of the belt when he heard a soft voice.

"Don't let go, Thad," the voice whispered in his ear. It was the voice he had heard earlier. "Reach...reach..." the voice said. Somehow he found the strength. Thad grabbed the belt even tighter with his hand and with all his might extended his free hand farther into the mud. Deeper under the mud he felt something hard, hard enough to gain leverage. He locked his fingers tight around the object and pulled.

He yelled at Rosie, "*Pull!*" With one final tug from Rosie, the two boys came crashing onto the riverbank, the hard object still gripped tightly in Thad's hand. Thad flipped over on his back to join Rosie as they both lay there, breathing like long-distance runners.

"You…saved…my life," Thad said between breaths.

"No way…I let you drown, man…" Rosie said, breathing just as heavily. "No way."

Marcus, Katey Jo, and Allie ran to their two soggy friends, overwhelmed at the miracle they just witnessed.

"Oh my God," Allie said. "Thad are you ok?" She fell to her knees on the wet ground beside him and ran her hand over his forehead and through his hair. "I thought you were going to drown." Tears formed in her eyes.

"Me, too," Thad replied with a nervous chuckle. "I'm ok. Are you ok? Did he hurt you anywhere?"

Allie smiled the biggest smile. Here was a boy who almost drowned, trying to save her from a terrible fate, and all he wanted to know was if she was ok. That moment, right then and there, was where Allie Thompson fell in love with Thad Taylor.

"I'm fine, Thad," she said, still smiling. "Thank you for helping me. That was the bravest thing I've ever seen." She looked at the other two boys. "And thank both of you. You saved me. I will never forget what you did."

Marcus blushed. He had never been the brave one. He was always too small to be the strong one. No, Marcus Pawley was always the funny one. But this time, he was one of the brave ones…and he liked it.

"Rosie, that was amazing," Katey Jo said.

"Yeah, man," Marcus added," if it weren't for you, we would have lost Thad."

Rosie was obviously embarrassed by the praise. He was the kind of guy who would do anything for anybody but not the kind who craved approval and gratitude.

Still catching his breath, he said, "I'm just glad he's out of the water. You guys check him out and make sure he's ok. I'm fine."

Marcus and Katey Jo joined Allie beside Thad.

"What's in your hand?" Katey Jo asked Thad.

"What?" Thad answered, confused. "I don't…"

Thad lifted his hand to see his fingers still grasping the object from the muddy bottom. The object that gave him enough anchorage to escape the deadly pull of the river. A bone. No one said anything as Thad turned the bone right and left, almost in disbelief.

"Is that what I think it is?" Marcus asked.

"It's a jawbone," Katey Jo answered. "A freaking human jawbone!"

Rosie hopped to his feet and looked at the object for himself. Katey Jo was right. There in Thad's hand was a jawbone, and it was definitely human. Rosie knew it when he saw it. Thad knew it when he saw it.

They both said in unison, "Abigail Lowery."

SQUISHY SHOES

The sun was just beginning to awaken the sky with its warm glow as the kids stared at the jawbone in Thad's hand. No one said anything for a brief moment, not even Marcus. Thad turned the jawbone from side to side, exposing its molars, bicuspids, canines, and incisors. The teeth appeared in good shape. There was only one silver filling and no other holes from decay.

"Whoever this was, they had good teeth," Katey Jo said.

"What do you mean 'whoever this was'?" Rosie said, looking up at Katey Jo. "This *is* Abigail Lowery."

"It could be," Katey Jo argued.

"It is," Rosie rebutted.

"He's right. It is Abigail," Thad said with a reassuring voice. "I know it is. It was downstream from where we found the necklace...plus..."

"Plus what?" Allie said, still kneeling next to Thad.

Thad was thinking of the voice he had heard in the water. He knew it was Abigail Lowery trying to help him so she could be found, but he also knew how crazy that sounded. "Nothing," he answered.

"Come on, Thad," Allie said, "tell us why you think it's Abigail." She placed a hand on his shoulder.

He just could not say no to Allie. "Plus....plus, she talked to me while I was in the river."

"What?" Katey Jo said, her hands on her hips.

The adrenaline was working its way out of Thad's and Rosie's system. The cold and wet was beginning to infuse their bodies with the shivers. The other kids could hear their teeth chatter, and the two wet boys hugged themselves to stay warm.

"I'm c-c-c-c-cold," Rosie said, both telling the truth and trying to change the subject. He did not want to talk about the voice he also heard. It worked...partially.

"Let's get back to the campsite," Marcus said. "The fire got messed up when that man fell into it, but I think there's enough of it still burning."

"The sun is coming up, too," Katey Jo added. "Soon you'll be begging to be cooler."

They started the short walk back to the campsite.

"Do you think that man is dead?" Allie asked.

"As a door nail," Katey Jo answered. "The current is too rough and too fast. They will find his body downstream somewhere."

"Should we tell the police?" Marcus asked. "About the man, I mean."

No one answered for a moment. Then Rosie said, "I say we tell them about everything. If we leave stuff out, it may sound made up. We won't get into trouble for that jerk. He's the one who held a knife to us, to Allie. As far as I'm concerned, he got what he deserved."

Allie and Katey Jo were worried about the punishment they would get for lying to their parents. But they realized that this was too big to try to sidestep around. They would all go to the police and just have to face the music with their folks.

The other kids agreed as they entered their ransacked campsite. Marcus's radio lay on its side. The melodies it had been playing were replaced with white noise. Abigail's pendant was on the ground near the spot where the man held Allie. Thad's camera had gone untouched, still sitting on the rock where he had placed it earlier to get their picture.

"Hey, here's Abigail's necklace," Rosie said, picking it up as he and Thad warmed themselves by what was left of the fire. He put it in his pocket.

The kids stood around the fire for a while, allowing their wet friends to warm up. The sun beamed and its rays injected heat into their bodies. Before long Thad and Rosie were no longer shaking and their hair was drying out.

Allie had stood by Thad the whole time. She reached her fingertips out and stroked his hand. He opened it to allow hers in, and they held hands while the fire and sun continued to work their magic.

"So what about those voices you heard?" Katey Jo said to Thad out of the blue.

Thad thought about how to say it so he didn't look crazy, but he didn't think that was possible, so he just let the truth spill out.

"When I was in the river, I thought I was going to drown. That's when she spoke to me. She told me to never give up and to reach for the belt."

No one said anything, so he continued. "And…I saw her face. She was beautiful, like an angel. I know it was Abigail."

Still, no one said anything. They all just looked at one another. Then Rosie spoke up.

"I heard her, too," Rosie said. "She told me to stand up and to pull."

After a moment, Allie said what everyone was thinking. "I believe you."

Katey Jo and Marcus nodded their heads in agreement.

"I think we should pray for her," Allie said.

"Good idea," Marcus said.

They kids made a circle and all held hands.

Allie prayed. "Dear God. Thank you for saving Thad and Rosie and for protecting us from the bad man last night. We think we have found Abigail Lowery's resting place. Please let her rest in peace and let her know we are going to help get her a proper grave. Amen."

They all said, "Amen."

They gathered up what was left of their scattered provisions and made their way back to town. Thad and Rosie brought up the rear, their shoes squishing with every step. Rosie hung back on purpose. He wanted to talk to Thad.

"That was crazy, man," Rosie said.

"I saw her, Rosie," Thad said. "I saw Abigail as clear as I see you right now. I recognized her from the newspaper microfiche."

"I believe you," Rosie said. "I heard her, too…crystal clear. Her voice was like she was right next to me." They both took a few more soggy steps. "She was trying to help us so we could find her."

"That's what I thought, too," Thad said.

"Well, we did find her," Rosie said. "I know it."

They walked a bit more without talking, and then Thad broke the silence.

"Thanks Rosie," he said. "I thought I was a goner. Thanks for doing that."

Rosie grabbed Thad by the arm and stopped him in his tracks. He looked him squarely in the eye.

"I told you: no way I let you drown, man, no way," he said.

Thad just smiled at him. He was thankful he had Rosie as a best friend. Big, strong, heart-of-gold Rosie.

The walk back to town took about an hour. The kids stood in front of the police station, plotting their next move. They decided to let Thad do the talking. He would tell everything as it happened, from the crazy man to falling in the river to finding the bone. They knew they were about to stir up a hornet's nest, but then again, sometimes hornets' nests needed stirring. They walked into the police station single file, Thad in the front, Rosie in the back, squishy shoes and all.

KICKING A HORNET'S NEST

Sergeant Kyle stirred his coffee. He grumbled at the small size of the plastic cup, but then raised his eyebrows as he took a sip. He liked the flavor.

"When did we get new coffee?" he asked no one in particular.

Starting his day like every other day, he made his way to his usual spot behind the front desk. "Assuming the position," as he liked to call it. He straightened papers he had piled on one side of the sturdy oak table and checked the ink in the pens stacked in an ornate pewter holder on the other side. Sure enough, one pen was dry. He eighty-sixed the Bic with a perfect three-point shot across the room into the garbage can.

"Score," he said with his hands raised, "and the crowd goes wild."

His hands still in the air, he saw the front door open through the corner of his eye. Five teenage kids walking into the station single file, on their own, is not something that happens every day in a police station. Recognizing two of the teenagers, he lowered his hands and picked up his coffee. Taking a sip, he motioned the kids to his desk.

"Well, good morning, Mr. Taylor," the sergeant said, placing his cup on the desk. "Just can't seem to get enough of us lately, can you?"

"Good morning, Sergeant Kyle," Thad said. "You remember Rosie, and this is Marcus, Allie, and Katey Jo."

"Kids," Sergeant Kyle said, bobbing his head. "What brings you back, Thad...and what happened to your eye?"

"Well, you know how we were asking about Abigail Lowery yesterday?" Thad asked.

"Yes?" The sergeant answered with a suspicious tone.

"Well, sir, we found her," Thad said.

"You found her?" The sergeant asked, half-surprised and half-unsure. "Just where did you find her?"

"The Cottonwood," Thad answered.

"You found the body of Abigail Lowery in the Cottonwood River?" Sergeant Kyle asked. He folded his arms like a disbelieving schoolteacher.

"Sort of," Thad said. "And we think a man drowned. It's a long story. Can we go back to the interrogation room and tell it to Chief Smitty?"

"Drowned?" Sergeant Kyle thought about what Thad was saying. If he was telling the truth, then a decades-old mystery could have just been solved. If he was mistaken or lying, then it would be a colossal waste of time—of the *chief's* time. Still, when you're talking about a kidnapping and murder case, and now a possible drowning, it was best to follow any and all leads. He was sure the kids were on a wild goose chase, but he decided to grant Thad's request.

He stood up and leaned his big, tall frame over the desk. To the kids he looked like a tree.

"Thad," he said with a measure of seriousness not to be trifled with, "if you are yanking my chain—"

"We're not." Thad stood his ground.

The sergeant shook his head and said, "Follow me."

He led the kids down the hallway and back into the same interrogation room they were in not twenty-four hours earlier. He told them to stay put and closed the door as he left the room.

Marcus slammed his hands down on the large table in the middle of the room and leaned in toward Katey Jo. "Where were you on the night of the fifth?" he said.

Katey Jo laughed. "Studying, alone…in my room!" she answered, putting her hands to her face, acting scared.

"Well, we know she's telling the truth," Allie said.

That brought a laugh from the entire group.

"Guys," Rosie said, "what we went through last night was something big. I mean it's gonna forever lock us together."

The kids looked at one another, knowing that Rosie was right. They were bound by something known only to those who stared death in the face and survived. No one said anything. The opening of the door broke their silence. Chief Smitty walked into the room, followed by Sergeant Kyle.

"Good morning, kids," the chief said, sitting down at the table across from Thad.

"Good morning," the teenagers said in unison. You could tell they had been indoctrinated with the routine at the public school system.

"Sergeant Kyle tells me you have information on the whereabouts of Abigail Lowery," the chief said.

Thad looked at Rosie and knew it was time to tell the story.

"Chief, I need to start at the beginning," he said.

"Let's hear it," Chief Smitty said as he folded his arms and leaned back in the chair.

Thad started with the repairing of the tire swing. He told them about the necklace they found on the tree branch in the Cottonwood. When Rosie pulled the pendant out of his pocket, you could see the growing interest of the police officers. Thad told them about the campout last night. When he got to the deranged man who held them at knifepoint, the chief asked Sergeant Kyle to take notes.

Thad told how the man was about to hurt Allie and how the boys tackled him. He told them that he and the man fell into the river, and the man got washed away. He was about mention the part about Abigail talking to him and Rosie, but he thought better of it. He described the man down to his bad teeth. The chief looked at Sergeant Kyle. The man Thad described matched the description of a man that had been mugging people in the area over the last few weeks. The believability factor continued to increase. Then Thad got to the part where he found the jawbone.

"Wait," the sergeant said, "you found a bone? A human jawbone?"

"It's definitely human," Katey Jo stated matter-of-factly.

"Thad," the chief said, "what you're telling us is one crazy story. It's not that I don't believe you; it's more like you've found something that's probably not what you think it is."

Thad just looked at the chief. He reached into his backpack and pulled out the jawbone. He laid it on the table in front of the policemen. The sergeant's mouth opened in disbelief. The chief picked up the bone and turned it side to side. That was it. That was what it took to kick the hornets' nest.

The station came alive. Cops ran here and there. They called the FBI. The phones rang. Dental records they had kept on file proved the teeth belonged to Abigail. Chief Smitty called the press to make an announcement that there were new leads in the cold case of Abigail Lowery. He had the kids by his side when he made the announcement.

The kids called their parents, who rushed down to the station, all except Mr. Pawley. But that was ok because Marcus called his uncle Mike, who showed up before anyone else.

The adults admonished them, saying, "You better not do that again," and "Are you crazy?" But all in all, the parents, and one uncle, were proud of what the children had accomplished.

It took the police only one day to find the rest of Abigail's body. She was buried near the tire swing on the bank of the river. The profilers figured that Abigail was the Cottonwood Killer's first victim, and he buried her to hide the evidence. As he became more aggressive, he would simply throw the bodies into the river. The high waters had begun to erode her grave, allowing some of her bones to wash downstream.

As for the man who invaded their campsite that night, a body was never found. No trace of the man was ever seen again. It was as if he just vanished, as if the devil really did call him home.

Abigail was buried in the cemetery next to her parents. The kids attended her funeral, as did Abigail's brothers, the police (with Chief Smitty and Sergeant Kyle in full dress), and the press, including the national news, who filmed the event. The kids were heroes and the mayor of Emporia announced they were going to "celebrate their doggedness and determination to bring Abigail to a peaceful resting place," by having a street dance on the last Friday night before the school year started.

Standing around Abigail's casket, the kids each said words before she was lowered into the ground. Thad reached for the necklace in his pocket and laid it on top of the casket. They left the funeral the same way they found Abigail, as a group. A group of friends that would remain that way until the end. Thad holding Allie's hand, Marcus leaning on Katey Jo, and Rosie, big Rosie, smiling ear to ear with his arm around Thad's shoulders.

A flash sparked as the press took their picture. Now that was a real "moment in time."

IT'S ABOUT TIME

Thad had stood on the front porch. The rocking chairs were dead-still in the crisp morning air. The sun was just making its way over the trees, quickly warming the porch. Thad held up the flowers and knocked on the heavy wooden door. He hurriedly checked his hair in the door's windowpane and was as satisfied as one could be in his present situation. The flowers were arranged beautifully, the purple petals standing in brilliant contrast to the white baby's breath. He quickly decided to hold them behind his back. His coat and tie were perfectly matched; a sharp look, but a little unusual for a warm summer day.

Allie opened the door, wearing an old terry cloth robe.

"Thad?" she said.

"Morning, Allie. I...uh, I just want to say..." He fumbled the words. "Um, what I mean...uh, can I come in?"

All that practice and I screw it up, he thought.

"Of course," she said, opening the door wide enough for him to enter.

The large mirror hanging in the foyer allowed guests to check themselves, which he did. The windowpane lied; his hair was sticking up in the back. He quickly licked his hand and patted it down when she turned to walk him into the kitchen.

He could smell the fresh paint on the cupboards. He usually was not a fan of red, but in here it looked good. Allie always had an eye for that sort of thing. She opened the cabinets and took out two coffee cups. She poured them both a cup from a pot she had began brewing minutes before he arrived. She didn't ask. She poured hers black and his with two sugars and one cream.

Thad watched. "You remembered," he said.

"I remember a lot of things," she said, smiling at him. She handed him the warm cup.

"These are for you," he said, handing her the bouquet and taking the coffee cup from her hands.

"Wild prairie roses," she said, sniffing the flowers, "my favorite. You remembered." Her smile was as beautiful as the first time he saw it.

"I remember a lot of things, too," he said, grinning back at her.

She placed the bouquet on the breakfast table and walked over to the counter.

"Allie, I'm sorry about yesterday," Thad started to say. "I shouldn't have been so harsh."

"No, Thad." Allie stopped him. "I shouldn't have acted like that. I was in shock with him barging in here and all. You were right; he is not in my life, and I need to let him go. And the more I thought about it, the more I realized you were protecting me. I've never had a man besides my father protect me. I didn't know how to react, I guess. But honestly, Thad, it felt good having you here when that happened. So what I should have said yesterday was... thank you."

"You are an amazing woman, Allie Thompson," Thad said, "and you damn sure don't need a man to protect you, but if anytime you ever call, I would be much obliged." He smiled at her and did his best Clark Gable.

She laughed and grabbed a picture frame on the counter and handed it to him. It held a photo of her with a wild prairie rose in her hair.

"Taken years ago by an amateur photographer," she said, smiling as she picked up her coffee cup.

"Wow, he really showed some talent," he said, chuckling. "He probably had a good future in the business."

"I wonder what he's doing now?" she said, sipping her coffee with both hands caressing the warm mug. She smiled a sexy smile and raised one eyebrow from behind the cup.

Thad knew the answer. He had always known the answer. There was no turning back, no second guessing. His fate was standing in front of him, smiling, wearing an old terry cloth robe, sipping freshly brewed coffee. *Life doesn't give you too many chances,* he thought. *When it lobs you a high, hanging fastball, you better take your best swing.* He had always tried to see the silver lining in things. Maybe Rosie was looking down from heaven right now, saying, "I had to go out in a Honda coming home from work, just so you could have another chance with her? You'd better not screw it up this time, you moron."

Thanks, Rosie, he thought. *I won't screw it up, brother.*

Looking at Allie, he answered, "He's standing in your kitchen, as nervous as he was all those years ago, telling you that he's hopelessly, totally, and completely in love with you. That he never stopped loving you and that if you will let him, he would love nothing more than to be with you...forever."

She put her cup down and looked back into his eyes. "It was always you, Thad. Always you."

They kissed each other with a passion that only love and time could build. Her lips felt like coming home. The years of emptiness disappeared, and Thad knew in that moment that everything had changed. He was tired of the lonely traveling, tired of the hotel beds and room service. He was where he needed to be, in the arms of the woman he loved, in the town where he was born.

"You know," he said, "I've been thinking about retiring and moving back home. Maybe opening up a photography studio."

"Really?" she said. "We could use a good photographer around here. Plus somebody's gotta take care of Marcus."

"Well, that's what Katey Jo—I'm sorry, Dr. McAnally—is for," he said.

They both laughed and kissed again. Making their way to the front porch, they sat in the rocking chairs and caught up, really caught up. They held hands and watched The Cottonwood River roll on by.

It was a hot day in Emporia, Kansas, but it was a good one.

EPILOGUE

Loved, Found and Not Forgotten

My bones grew old without me. My flesh disappeared with the changes of the seasons. I laid in a muddy grave longer than I breathed air. Still, I did not give up the fight. I did not give in to the darkness. I knew my time would come. The evil that took my life came and went but I persevered. I could hear him scream when he stepped into the darkness. I laughed when the demons pulled him under, into the forever night.

The sound of The Cottonwood River rushing by helped to pass the time. It was like a friend, encouraging me to never quit. The river became my protector. Many were the days I could feel the current working on the walls of my grave, inching closer and closer to my remains, like a rescuer with a shovel trying to free me from my prison.

The day I felt the water rush over me, I knew it wouldn't be long. Down the river parts of me went. I knew the children from Emporia would find me. I came to them when I could. I used all of my strength and energy to help guide them toward me. They were brave and strong. I heard their promise in the flickering of the firelight, and they honored that promise.

Now I rest beside my parents. I saw the children stand around my new grave. I saw the one named Thad lay my necklace on my coffin. I will forever be grateful.

Abigail Lowery, loved, found and not forgotten.

Made in the USA
Charleston, SC
27 February 2015